**Taxi 1**

"If you like your mystery with a paranormal edge, then you should be reading this series." ~Cheryl Green

**Praise for Renaissance Faire Mysteries**

"**Fatal Fairies** was a good read. I loved being back at the Renaissance Faire Village with Jessie, Chase and all of the village characters. I like the magical twist that happens to Jessie in this book and I'm curious to see what other magic happens in future books. Thank you Joyce and Jim for writing a great story that transported me to a village I wouldn't mind living in! Eagerly awaiting the next book in the series!" ~ **R. Davila**

Praise for Missing Pieces Mysteries

"I really enjoyed **A Watery Death**, it was full of a few surprises and a very nice guest appearance that was fun to read about. As well as a nice surprise but sad guest appearance to enjoy. Can't wait for the next book!" ~ **April Schilling**

*Praise for the Retired Witches Mysteries*

"**Spell Booked** kept me guessing. Who was good, who could be trusted, and who was the rogue witch? Joyce and James Lavene created a world where magic and mundane live together yet separate-even in the same households." ~ **Cozy Up With Kathy**

Some of our other series:

*Renaissance Faire Mysteries*
Wicked Weaves
Ghastly Glass
Deadly Daggers
Harrowing Hats
Treacherous Toy
Perilous Pranks—Novella
Murderous Matrimony
Bewitching Boots

*Missing Pieces Mysteries*
A Timely Vision
A Touch of Gold
A Spirited Gift
A Haunting Dream
A Finder's Fee
Dae's Christmas Past
A Watery Death

*Taxi for the Dead Mysteries*
Undead by Morning
Broken Hearted Ghoul
Dead Girl Blues

*Retired Witches Mysteries*
Spell Booked
Looking for Mr. Good Witch

*A Canterville Book Shop Mystery*
A Dickens of a Murder

# Murder Fir Christmas

A Christmas Tree Valley Mystery

By

Joyce and Jim Lavene
With
Chris Lavene

Book coach and editor—Jeni Chappelle
**http://www.jenichappelle.com/**

Acknowledgments:
The authors want to acknowledge Patricia Tucker for her help in choosing the name for the wolf in this book, Cynthia Chappelle for whom Bonnie Tuttle's new life was inspired by.

Also Jeni Chappelle and Emily Andreis for their help or this book would not have been finished.

**Dedication:**

In loving memory of Joyce Lavene who passed away on October 20, 2015

We will miss her and hope her memory and works live on as she would want them to.

## Chapter One

Bonnie Tuttle braked abruptly for the tiny, old man in the white robe. He appeared out of nowhere and was standing in the middle of the road with a greenwood staff in one hand. The other hand rested on the side of the biggest stag she'd ever seen. The antlers had sixteen points. The man's long, white hair whipped around his aged Cherokee face as the stag pawed at the blacktop.

She didn't turn off the truck engine since she wasn't sure it would start again, but she got out to address the man. Old snow was heaped on the sides of the road where it had been pushed by a plow, and salt grated under her tennis shoes. The area had readied itself for another snowstorm.

"Excuse me, sir." The wind whipped at her short, sun-bleached blond hair and her jacket that had been adequate when she'd left Alabama. "It's not a good idea to stand in the road. Why don't you come with me and we'll find out where you belong?"

"Unega Awinita." He bowed his head elegantly toward her. "I have awaited your return. Welcome home. We have great need of your presence."

She started to speak, but the man and the stag were gone. It was as though they disappeared right before her eyes. A few snow flurries swirled around her as she scanned the nearby woods for any sign of them.

Bonnie rubbed her eyes. She was more tired than she thought. Good thing she was close to town. What was that he'd called her?

She got back in her pickup, glancing around one last time before she headed into Sweet Pepper, Tennessee.

It was two weeks before Christmas, and the small town was decorated with plenty of holly—both fake and real. There was a huge Douglas fir tree at the VFW Park in the center of town decorated with lights and gleaming, colored ornaments.

She parked in front of town hall, glad to turn off the engine that had been overheating for the last fifty miles. She hadn't been sure if the old truck would make it from Alabama, but she was finally here.

A cold wind swept down from the Great Smoky Mountains that surrounded the town, and she shivered, not used to the colder temperatures anymore. She was originally from this area—Christmas Tree Valley, just past Sweet Pepper and down the mountain. But she hadn't lived here in ten years. Her visits were during the summer when it was warm. She'd forgotten how cold it could be or that there could be so much snow.

Bonnie hurried into the warmth of the building. Snow, ice, and cold were going to take some getting used to, but since her job was primarily outside as a Federal

Wildlife Agent, she'd get used to it pretty quickly. A new coat would help. Maybe some boots besides her rubber wading boots would be good too.

"Good morning!" A woman with teased-high, fifties hair, dressed as though she'd never left that era, greeted her. "Can I help you?"

Bonnie looked around. There were plenty of people moving back and forth, in and out of the offices. She didn't recognize any of them. Even though Christmas Tree Valley was the next town over, she hadn't grown up here. This was somewhere her mother shopped once in a while, and they always came to the Sweet Pepper Festival. But that brief acquaintance didn't help now. She was still a stranger.

"I'm Bonnie Tuttle." She pushed at her hair that had a tendency to swing into her face and pulled out her federal ID. Maybe it would've been better to wear the uniform. "I'm here to meet with Chief Don Rogers and Agent Harvey Shelton. Could you tell them I'm here?"

The woman behind the desk got up and smiled. "Well aren't you a tall drink of water! You're going to get along just fine with our fire chief, Stella Griffin. At least you two will see eye to eye, if you'll forgive the joke."

At slightly over six feet, Bonnie was used to being taller than most women and quite a few men. She nearly always felt as though she was towering over everyone.

"Thank you." She was really tall compared to this woman who offered her hand.

"Sandie Selvy. It's very nice to meet you." She patted her slightly stiff hair. "Let me find out where they're going to hold this shindig. I'll be right back."

"Nice to meet you, Miss Selvy."

"Just call me Sandie. We'll be seeing a lot of each other since you're taking Harvey's place. It's very exciting to have another woman involved in town business."

Bonnie started to correct her. She had nothing to do with town business besides the formalities of working with the police and sheriff from time to time. Mostly she spent her days giving wildlife education classes and in the woods and on the lakes. In Alabama, that included a lot of swamps too. The weather was warmer, and there were plenty of gators.

Here she knew it would be black bears, deer, bobcats, and such, with a helping of rattlesnakes on the side.

A tall woman who equaled her height came into the building. Her fiery red hair was pulled back in a ponytail. She wore jeans and a heavy jacket with a Sweet Pepper Fire Brigade T-shirt under it. This had to be Stella Griffin, the fire chief.

She looked tough, despite the freckles and curious, brown eyes. She glanced aside for a moment and said a few words to an empty place beside her. As soon as she noticed Bonnie, she moved forward and stretched out her hand.

"You must be the new Wildlife Agent. I'm Stella Griffin. Welcome to Sweet Pepper."

Her accent wasn't from Tennessee or anywhere in the South. But her smile was as warm as her hearty handshake.

"Bonnie Tuttle. Nice to meet you. You must be the fire chief. Miss Selvy said we'd see eye to eye. I know what she means now."

Stella laughed. "Yeah. Like you didn't have enough

jolly green giant jokes growing up, right? But Sandie's nice. And she won't bring it up all the time. It's probably hard for someone as short as she is to constantly look up."

"I suppose that's true." Bonnie already liked Stella. It wasn't just the height thing either. She hoped they'd be friends. She wasn't sure how many of those she had left in this area.

Harvey Shelton came out of an office accompanied by another man. When she saw the shield on his belt, she assumed this was Chief Rogers. He was in his fifties, she guessed, with pale blue eyes and graying, blond hair cut in a flat top.

"You made it right on time and before the snowstorm they're predicting." Harvey shook her hand. He had bushy, dark brows and brown eyes, and his dark mustache wasn't quite centered on his face, a curiosity she had noticed when she'd met him in Alabama. "Welcome. This is Chief Don Rogers of the Sweet Pepper Police Department. Chief, this is the very hard working and astute young woman who is taking my place so I can retire—Agent Bonnie Tuttle."

They shook hands. Chief Rogers seemed to want to sum her up in a glance.

"Welcome to Sweet Pepper," he said. "I see you've already met our fire chief. Let's take this in the conference room. We have a lot to cover."

It was easy to tell during the briefing that the Sweet Pepper Police Department had a much closer relationship with Harvey than Bonnie had enjoyed with the police departments in the area she'd been responsible for in Alabama. She guessed it was because the mountainous area was sparsely populated compared to the many small towns where she'd worked.

Even though Federal Wildlife Agents were able to investigate almost any crime in their jurisdiction, knowing she had backup that was closer than the next state didn't bother her. She'd worked mostly on her own but welcomed the assistance where ever she could get it.

At the end of the meeting, she gave her cell number to the fire and police departments, who gave her their information as well. She had a bag full of brochures and Welcome to the Community coupons and notepads for her refrigerator. The people seemed happy to have her here.

"I understand you still have relatives in Christmas Tree Valley and Sweet Pepper," Chief Rogers said as the meeting was breaking up.

"Yes. I'm actually here to help my mother. She lives in the valley. She hasn't been well for the past few years."

"I'm sorry I have to ask, but who is that?"

She smiled. That was one thing that never changed. If you lived in a small town, everyone wanted to know everything about you.

"Her name is Rose Tuttle now, but she was Rose Addison growing up. She was raised right here in Sweet Pepper."

The lights in the town hall flickered, and the front door blew open. A gust of air carried papers from desks to the floor.

"Might be that storm coming this way." Harvey glanced around the room.

Stella turned her head to the side again and muttered a few words before looking back. She appeared to be upset about something more than some flickering and the door coming open. She wondered if the fire chief had some issues—talking to herself being one of them.

"I've met your mother," Stella said. "I didn't realize she was in bad health. I'm sorry."

Since these people were recent acquaintances, Bonnie thanked her but didn't go into detail about her mother's health. "My brother, Eric, has taken an overseas position in Germany with his company. It's not a big deal."

It had been a big deal leaving her friends in Alabama, but she understood that her brother couldn't pass up the opportunity. And maybe it was good for her to start again. She'd thought a relationship she'd cultivated was going somewhere, but it seemed she'd been mistaken. Saul Chase wasn't ready to settle down.

"Well, you let us know if we can do anything to help," Chief Rogers said. "We're family here in Sweet Pepper and Christmas Tree Valley. We work together."

Bonnie thanked him and gathered everything together. Sandie gave her a canvas Sweet Pepper tote bag to carry it in. She walked toward the door to leave, and it opened unexpectedly. What was even stranger was that it closed behind her. They obviously needed someone to fix that door.

Harvey came out right after her. He was laughing as he put on his uniform hat. "I think it's official. Eric Gamlyn likes you."

She thought back to the group of people she'd been introduced to. She didn't remember anyone by that name. "I'm sorry. Was he there? Is he the mayor or something?"

He kept laughing. "No. Sorry. You're not exactly

from here, so you don't recognize the name. He's the former fire chief. He's kind of famous, so everyone knows him."

"I still don't remember him. There weren't that many people in the room, but it was a long drive."

"You probably wouldn't have seen him. He's been dead for about forty years. I only know a lot about him from his folklore. But Stella lives with him full time. If she says she met your mother, so did Eric."

"A ghost?" She was having trouble with that. Not that the valley didn't have ghosts. They had ghosts in Alabama too. But usually people didn't talk about them like they were right here. "Is this some kind of initiation?"

"No. I expect it's a lot to take in, especially on your first day. Let's go down to the Sweet Pepper Cafe and grab some lunch. We can talk about getting everything set up before I leave."

She remembered the cafe. The smell of hush puppies and fried chicken drifted down the street with the last brown leaves of autumn and a few snow flurries. There was nothing to worry about yet. She had plenty of time to eat.

They got settled in around a table, and a young woman who looked like she was in high school came to take their orders. Everyone stopped by to say hello to Harvey and was introduced to Bonnie. She was sure she'd know the entire town before she left. There was friendly—and then there was Sweet Pepper.

"Naturally you'll take the Hummer. The government bought that for us a few years back. It will get in and out of anything." Harvey added sugar to his coffee. "There's the house too, but you said you don't want that. I've arranged to rent it out through a real estate company so you won't have to bother with it. The office is right next door. I've already taken my stuff out of there. The basics are still in there—chair, desk, telephone, and fax. I'll give you the information to get in touch with whoever you need from the feds."

"Thanks. I've never moved around like this, so I appreciate the help."

"You've been in Alabama since you started?"

"Yes. You were already established here when I finished training, and you didn't seem ready to move to something else."

"I wasn't then, but I've been doing this for the last thirty years. I'm ready to retire." He laughed.

"That's understandable."

The waitress brought back their meals, both with hushpuppies. Bonnie had gone for the chicken rather than the fish as Harvey had. No offense, but there was no way they could make fish like they did in Alabama.

"Why didn't you tell them that your mother has Alzheimer's? You might need their help with her sometime."

"I don't know. I'm not used to sharing personal information with people I barely know."

"Don't worry. You'll get used to it. That's the way folks are around here. I thought you'd know that, being from here and all."

"Sometimes they're a little too friendly," she muttered.

They heard fire engines coming down Main Street. Everyone in the cafe stopped to speculate as to what was going on.

A police officer rushed into the cafe, quickly

scanning the tables until he found us. "Harvey, some fool started a fire out on the little island in Sweet Pepper Lake. The chief wants to know if you'll come out there to help."

"Sure, Skeet. This is my replacement, Agent Bonnie Tuttle."

"Rose Tuttle's daughter?" the plump, balding officer asked. "Pleased to meet you, ma'am."

"Let's get going," Harvey said to her as he pushed away from the table. "Never a dull moment."

## Chapter Two

She left her pickup at the curb and got in the Hummer with Harvey. She didn't know what she expected from the vehicle—she'd never ridden in one. But it operated smoothly, even though it took up half the narrow streets in the downtown area.

Sweet Pepper Lake was one place Bonnie remembered. She'd spent many sunny afternoons out there on the beach when she was in high school. It looked just as she remembered it, with the tall mountains ringing it. The cloud cover was hanging low on the mountaintops, making the water appear as gray as the sky. The wind was colder here, coming off the lake with no trees to slow it down.

Both fire engines as well as two police cars were at the shore. A large boat outfitted with hoses and a water cannon was at the dock. It looked as though it was ready to leave.

"We have our boat docked over here by theirs," Harvey said as we got out of the Hummer. "We don't have the water power they have, but we have more maneuverability since we have to get in and out of the coves and up close by the dam to check fishing permits."

Bonnie followed him to a HydraSports boat, and they jumped onboard. It was much nicer than the boats she was used to in Alabama. Clearly there was more money in the area that was allotted to the agency. She untied the boat as Harvey got on the helm. The fireboat, *Tennessee Teardrop*, was almost to the little island before they were on the water.

Smoke from the fire added to the heavy clouds. The air was full of it, playing havoc with their noses as they got closer.

"I see someone on the shore," she said. "Something must've happened to his boat."

"I see him. Radio the *Teardrop* that we'll pick him up. I'd like the opportunity to kick his butt for being so stupid. It's always dry this time of year. Everyone knows that."

The driver of the fireboat, Rufus Palcomb, let her know that they'd spotted a fishing boat off the side of the island that appeared to be adrift. "We're dispatching another boat to get it. Chief says not to bother you with that since there are so many animals on the island that need rescuing."

"Copy that," she replied. "We're almost there."

Harvey brought the boat in close to the shore, and the man, rifle in hand, waded into the water to climb aboard.

"My boat got away from me," he told them. "Can we go pick it up?"

"Someone else is taking care of that," Bonnie told him. "Do you have a permit for that rifle, sir?"

"Permit? I live in Sweet Pepper. Why do I need a permit?"

"You were hunting, weren't you?"

"Only a few ducks." He shrugged. "I wasn't hunting deer or anything."

"You still need a permit, son," Harvey told him. "What's your name?"

He took out his driver's license and handed it to Bonnie. "Ray Hoy, sir. I'd really appreciate it if we could get my boat before it drifts further away."

"We're not doing that right now, Mr. Hoy." She wrote down his name and address. "But someone will pick it up. I'll have to confiscate that rifle. It's not duck hunting season, and you don't have a permit. Is it registered?"

"No, ma'am. My daddy says only communists register their weapons."

There was a call from the *Teardrop*. "Royce Pope has the boat. Is your man named Fletcher Bancroft?"

"No." She glanced at his driver's license again. "Ray Hoy."

Rufus laughed. "Better hold him for the sheriff then. I don't think this is his boat."

Bonnie had only used her handcuffs a handful of times in the past ten years. She took them out and told him to turn around. "I'm placing you under arrest, sir, for several wildlife violations as well as possibly stealing a boat. Just take a seat, and we'll get this settled."

He sat where she put him. She pocketed his license with the first paperwork.

"Don't forget we've got him for this fire too,"

Harvey said. "This is our jurisdiction out of the city. If it was a structure fire, it would be different."

"Sure. Thanks."

There was an old dock on the island. It was enough to tie the boat up to but not enough to use to get on land. Bonnie and Harvey jumped into the thigh-high water with their nets and snares to save what animals they could by getting them off the island.

A third splash followed as Ray Hoy pushed himself backwards off the boat. Bonnie realized that she should have cuffed him to the railing and not trusted that he'd stay where she put him.

"I'll get him," she told Harvey, red-faced after she'd made a rookie mistake on her first day.

"Don't take all day about it," her partner said in an irritated voice. "This place is going up quick."

She looked at the burning treetops. The smoke was heavier now as the forest on the island was consumed. She could only guess that there were a couple of acres out here. She'd been out there as a kid—they all had—but never paid any attention.

The water cannons from the *Tennessee Teardrop* were blasting at the fire as she dove into the cold water. It was one heck of a welcome.

Bonnie made quick movements into the water, knowing Ray Hoy couldn't have gotten far in this cold water—or with his hands cuffed together either. She circled the boat, watching for him, and came up for air near the old dock. Taking a deep breath, she was about to go down again when she noticed her quarry. He was close to the dock, as though hoping she wouldn't notice him there.

Looking to surprise him so she wouldn't have to

chase him again, she came around from the other side of the dock, put out one hand to grab him by the shoulder, and surfaced. He didn't move or try to get away.

"Let's try this again," she said as she surfaced with him, using her other hand to grab the cuffs on his wrists. No way he was slipping out of his jacket and trying to get away.

She expected some kicking and thrashing right away and then pleading and debating once they were out of the water. To her surprise, the first part didn't happen. But he also didn't get to his feet, even though they were close enough to shore. She grabbed the front of his jacket. He was limp in her hold. She dragged him to shore, his feet still in the water.

There was a bright red wound in his chest, still bleeding. He'd been shot.

Confused, wondering if he'd taken his rifle and shot himself for one long moment, Bonnie dragged him further up on the shore. She checked his pulse—there was none. He was dead.

"I need immediate response from an EMS unit," she shouted into the radio. "Our suspect has been shot. No pulse."

"We'll get someone to you as soon as they can," Rufus shouted back.

"I can't stay with him," she returned, looking at the inferno the woods on the island had become. "Any word from Harvey?"

"Negative," Rufus said. "If you can get in there and do any good, I'd say leave Hoy and do what you can. It doesn't sound like he's going anywhere."

Bonnie got her gear together and put on a mask to protect her lungs from the heated smoke. They didn't carry scuba gear as the fire department did, but it should be enough. There was no point in her trying to get in the burning zone. The animals that had survived would be long gone.

She called Harvey as she bagged two possums. She left them on the shore where she could easily put them in the boat and get away quickly if needed. There was no response from her partner. She hoped he hadn't gone in too close to the center of the fire.

Several raccoons ran out, and she put on her heavy gloves to pick them up. They were almost overcome with smoke, so they were docile. Again she left them where she could grab them on the way out.

There was a gunshot that brought her head up from what she was doing. It was loud, probably a shotgun, to be heard over the roar of the fire. She called Harvey again. There was still no response. A group of rabbits were directly in her path. She scooped them up and ran back to the shore with them.

Despite wanting to save as many animals as she could, she had to go after Harvey. As far as she knew, he was the only one on the island with a gun. It could be that Ray Hoy had a hunting partner. She watched a hundred ducks fly away from the trees, some with their feathers smoking, but they seemed all right if they could make shore on the other side of the lake.

"Harvey?" she yelled against the force of the strong wind generated by the fire. She followed the path that led along the shore. He couldn't be in the woods. There was no point in searching for him there. She saw a dozen field mice get to safety floating on a piece of wood.

She used the radio again and again, calling to her partner. He didn't reply. When she found him face down at the edge of the woods, she knew why. Rushing to him, she turned him over.

There was a bullet wound in his head. There was no point in checking for a pulse. Harvey was dead.

An animal growled at her—a young wolf. His coat was covered in sand where he must have rolled to put out the fire on his fur. He'd been burned. His eyes were glued on her, watching her every move. There was also blood on his side, as though he'd cut himself in his haste to get away.

She called Rufus to confirm Harvey's death and gave him specific details on where he could be found. Though she knew she shouldn't do it and some medical examiner would have her head, Bonnie moved his body to the edge of the water so there was no danger of him being burned. She hadn't known him long, but common decency dictated that she preserve his body as well as she could for his family. The crime scene was a mess anyway. She was willing to take the lumps for her actions.

Dozens of small animals still streamed out of the woods toward the water. Two skunks waddled by. She was grateful that they were in too much of a hurry to raise their tails. One long black snake slithered close to the water then backed away before taking the plunge. He followed a zigzag pattern along the edge until she couldn't see him anymore.

The wolf was still in the same place, not even ten yards from where she was beside Harvey. He looked hungry. His body was thin and his eyes ferocious. He wasn't growling anymore. She thought he might not have the strength for it. If he was weak to begin with, he might be in shock. Normally a single wolf, especially a pup, would run off when he saw a human.

Finally the smaller boat that had come with the fire brigade reached her. The medical examiner wasn't with the two firemen who were unknown to her, but they insisted that they had permission to move the body.

"You won't mind if I confirm that, will you?" she asked, taking out her radio.

"No. I'm Allen Wise, and this is Tagger Reamis. You can call Chief Griffin or Rufus is on the radio on the *Teardrop*. You must be the new Wildlife Agent. Welcome to Sweet Pepper."

The older man put out his hand to shake hers. Rufus answered her call and told her the two men should be there. "They'll take Harvey and Ray to the coroner's office. Don't worry about it. Finish up what you're doing and get off the island as soon as you can."

Bonnie would have to remember that in Tennessee they had coroners. In Alabama they had medical examiners. Just one of a thousand things she'd have to get used to—that and bossy firemen. She wasn't used to being told what she should do.

"Sorry." She shook hands with Allen and Tagger. "I know things can get weird with handling bodies. I believe this may be a murder rather than an accident. I guess we'll have to see what shakes loose when the fire is out."

They all looked up at the flames, which had mostly been quenched by the heavy water from the fire boat. It was still hot and smoldering in the dry leaves from the fall. They could catch on again easily in those conditions.

As she was looking up, the first few flakes of snow from the promised winter storm fell delicately on her face. Snow would help put out the fire. Any moisture was better than none.

The two men covered Harvey's body with a tarp, carefully lifted it to the boat, and then did the same with Ray's.

"Don't wait too long out here," Tagger said with a grin. "We don't want to lose you too."

"Thanks. I'll get off the island as soon as I can."

She took the animals she'd captured and put them in her boat. When she looked back along the shore, the young wolf was still waiting there. He'd finally laid down on the gravel and sand.

Bonnie wasn't sure if he could make the swim to the mainland. She didn't relish being gnawed by him, although she'd had her rabies shot and wasn't afraid of that. The snow kept falling, now mixed with some freezing rain. The wolf didn't move, and it started to cover him as it did the rocks and shrubs along the water.

Common sense told her to leave him there and he'd find a way back on his own. Compassion and a great love of all animals made her get out of the boat and approach him again. That love was the reason she'd become a Wildlife Agent.

"Let's not make both of us sorry that I'm doing this." She took off her jacket and crept closer to the wolf. He looked up at her with intelligence and pain in his eyes. "I'm Bonnie. Maybe you can introduce yourself later. Right now, we should get off the island. I hope that's okay with you."

The wolf closed his eyes as she wrapped her coat around his ragged body. He barely weighed anything as she lifted him gently. His breath came out as a mixture of pants and growls.

"Trust me. No one is going to hurt you now. Just lay

back and enjoy the ride."

## Chapter Three

The lake water was so cold that the snow and ice stuck to the surface. Already the boat was glazed with it. The *Tennessee Teardrop* still waited by the island even though the water cannon and hoses were off. A group of five firefighters that included Chief Griffin started into the woods with axes and shovels. They'd have to make sure the fire was completely out before they left. She didn't envy them their job.

The *Teardrop* was big enough to navigate anything but a frozen lake. Bonnie's boat was in good shape but didn't care for the thickness of the water. She kept her focus on the boat reaching the dock on the other side of the lake. The wolf was quiet where she put him in a small pocket between the boat wall and the seat. She'd carefully kept him away from the other animals even though they were in sacks. She knew he could still smell them.

The snow was falling much harder by the time she reached the dock and secured the boat. Putting on her elbow-high, leather gloves again to protect her hands and forearms, she carefully let the animals she'd captured out on land. They ran off quickly, although the possum had a few snarky complaints about his treatment.

The little wolf wasn't doing as well. He wasn't unconscious, but he was barely breathing and didn't move or growl when she picked him up in her jacket. Before covering the boat to protect it from the storm, Bonnie realized that her truck was still in town. When she couldn't find the keys to the Hummer in the boat, she assumed Harvey had them.

She thought about calling the fire brigade for help after the boat was protected, but with firefighters still on the island, there wasn't much they could do to help. She had to get back to town and get the wolf to a vet.

All the lines were busy at the police switchboard. Probably with weather-related issues. Bonnie saw a man setting up his boat for the storm too. There was a big, black pickup nearby, the only one in the parking lot. She got the wolf in her arms again and walked over to ask for a ride.

"Excuse me," she hailed him. "I'm Bonnie Tuttle with the Federal Wildlife Agency. I need a ride into town to get my pickup. Would you mind taking me there?"

She could commandeer his vehicle, but this wasn't the kind of emergency the agency meant for that power. Her partner's death was going to be hard enough to explain—especially on her first day—she didn't want to explain that she took this man's truck to save a wolf's life.

He looked up at her from under his cowboy hat. "I'll be glad to take you into town, Agent. I'm Matthew Brown Elk." He shook her hand. "What's that you've got?"

"A wolf pup. He was on the island during the fire. I'm hoping to get him to a vet in time."

Matthew nodded toward the Hummer. "Is that not yours?"

It had the insignia of the Federal Wildlife Agency on the door, of course. She knew he must think she was a complete idiot.

"Something happened to my partner on the island. He has the keys. I'm sorry to rush you, but can we go now?"

He clearly wasn't the rushing type. She watched him impatiently as he thought about her story, at least that was what she thought he was doing.

"There's no vet around here that's gonna take a wolf. Dalmatians and kittens, but no wild animals."

"Can you just give me a ride into town? I'll take it from there. Thanks."

"Sure. I can take you to the vet's office, if you like. Maybe you can convince them that a wolf would be a safe patient."

She stared into his dark eyes. His face had features from a Native American heritage, maybe Cherokee. They were still standing in the snow, large flakes falling on them. The roads were probably getting hazardous. She knew the road into Christmas Tree Valley got icy and dangerous quickly. It might already be too late to get out of Sweet Pepper.

"Thanks. But I can find someone who'll help me with the wolf. All I need is a ride back to town." *Right now*, she wanted to add but didn't.

"I can give you a hand with him. I've worked on wolves before. I'm not a vet, but I might be your best bet in this case."

Her radio went off at the same time as her cell phone. Her phone was in her jacket pocket and the radio was on her belt. With her hands full holding the wolf, she couldn't reach either one.

"Shall I?" he asked.

She almost said no. He had laughing eyes. She never trusted men who smiled too much. But it might be someone who could actually offer her a quick ride into town. Maybe the fire brigade members who'd left with Harvey's body had come back.

"Sure. The radio, please." She shivered as a strong gust of wind blew off the lake. At least the wolf was warm in her jacket.

It was Chief Rogers wanting to know what was going on. "I've got Harvey Shelton's body under a tarp in my office, Agent Tuttle. The road was already impassable going to Pigeon Forge. I need you back here to answer some questions about what happened out there."

"The keys for the Hummer are with Harvey," she told him as her companion held the button for her to speak. "I'm still at the lake and trying to find a ride back, Chief."

"I'm here too," Matthew said into the radio. "I'll bring Agent Tuttle back with me, Don. We'll be there as soon as we can."

"Is that you, Brown Elk? All right then. You should be able to get her back here. Thanks."

"Chief, I—" But she'd missed her opportunity. Chief

Rogers was done, leaving her to the same problem she already had. Great.

"Look." She could see being nice about this wasn't working. "I need to get this wolf somewhere he can be treated. Can you do that in a short amount of time, or do I need to take your truck and do it myself?"

He grinned. "You can try. The last person who wanted to take it ended up unconscious in the street. I don't think that's a good way to begin our friendship. I've worked with Agent Shelton. He was a good man but not much of a tracker."

"Okay." She closed her eyes and asked for patience. "Can we go now?"

"Sure. Let me get the door." He clipped her radio back to her belt. "Are you sure you don't want me to answer your phone too? That might be annoying to the wolf. I know it's annoying me."

"Let's just get in the truck and go back to town. I can answer it as we go."

He opened the passenger door and helped her in so she wouldn't have to let go of the wolf. He didn't waste any time getting to the driver's side and starting the engine.

Bonnie's phone started ringing again. It was her mother.

"Where are you?" she asked. "There's a big storm coming. You might have to stop in town before you get here. The road into the valley might be closed."

"Don't worry, Mom. I'll be fine. I'm in Sweet Pepper now. Has Eric left yet?"

"No. His plane was delayed due to the bad weather. Do you want to talk to him?"

"That's okay." She was very conscious of the other

man listening to her. "I'll get there as soon as I can."

"Be careful, Bonnie. I know how you hate driving in snow."

"That was a long time ago. I'll be fine. Don't worry." She ended the call and put the phone in her pocket. She was relieved to hear the wolf growl faintly.

"So, you're a native coming home." Matthew grinned but kept his eyes on the slippery road. "And you live in Christmas Tree Valley. That's a coincidence. I do too. You must be Rose Tuttle's girl that she always talks about. No wonder you're shivering since you're used to that Alabama climate."

Bonnie clamped her teeth together to keep them from chattering. "I also had a refreshing swim in the lake trying to catch the man who started the fire."

"Why didn't you say so?" He turned on the heat in the truck. "Did you get him?"

"Yes. But someone was out there with a rifle. He shot Ray Hoy and Harvey."

"Seriously?" The truck tires slid off the road a few feet, but he recovered them. "Harvey and Ray are both dead? Who'd want to kill them?"

"No doubt Harvey had some enemies as a Wildlife Agent." She shrugged, highly aware of her cold, wet clothes and shoes. "Or it was a mistake. I'm not sure. Ray might've had help with the fire and his partner didn't want anyone to know he was involved."

"I could see that. Arson is punishable with prison time." He mulled the matter over. "It could've been Vince Stookey. Those two are always together."

"Thanks. I'll check that out."

Though it was a slippery, dangerous ride back into Sweet Pepper, they finally made it. Matthew parked the truck on the street, and Bonnie got ready to go inside to talk to Chief Rogers.

"I'll take the wolf," he said. "Trust me. If anyone can fix him, I can. Ask Don when you go inside."

She was between a rock and a hard place. She knew time was valuable as far as finding Harvey's killer. That was no doubt her primary effort in this, and yet she didn't want to leave the young wolf without help. He could die while she answered questions and drew diagrams.

He held out his arms. "I won't hurt him. I promise."

Bonnie had no choice. She gave him the wolf, still wrapped in her jacket. "Take good care of him."

"You want your jacket?" He peered into the warm cocoon she'd created for the animal. "Maybe not. Here, take him back a minute."

She took the wolf back, wondering if he'd changed his mind about tending to him. Instead, Matthew took off his heavy jacket and put it around her shoulders. It hung down almost to her knees and ballooned around her, still carrying his warmth and scent.

"Thanks," she said awkwardly. "But what will you do?"

"I'll be fine. Give me the wolf. Good luck trying to explain what happened. Call me when you're finished."

"I don't have your cell phone number."

He rattled off his number, and she quickly punched it into her phone. He had the wolf and her jacket. It seemed the day was doomed to be full of surprises—most of them unpleasant.

She felt stupid walking into town hall wearing a coat that was too big for her, but she'd finally stopped shivering. She wasn't taking it off to appease any small-town questions.

There were a few unusual looks when she got inside, but no one said anything about it. Sandie rushed to get her a towel and a cup of hot coffee. Bonnie felt even worse about dripping on the floor. At least it was tile so it would clean up easily.

"That's Brown Elk's jacket, isn't it?" Chief Rogers stalked from his office. "You look rough. I can lend you a dry uniform if that would help."

Embarrassed, she told him she'd go out and get some dry clothes before they talked. "Sorry. I had a wolf in my arms and didn't want to put him down. Matthew is looking after it."

"He's the best we've got," the chief confirmed. "You stay put. John will take care of that for you." He turned to a tall man with brown hair who was wearing an officer's uniform. "Will you get Agent Tuttle something dry to wear?"

John Trump stared at him. "Sir?"

"My blue suitcase in the front seat," she told him, fishing her keys out of her wet pocket. "Thanks, Officer Trump. I'm Agent Bonnie Tuttle. Nice to meet you."

He shook her hand. "Nice to meet you too, ma'am. I'm sorry this had to be your first day in Sweet Pepper. We don't have many murders around here."

"I guess I just got lucky to catch two of them on the same day." She smiled weakly. "I've always been lucky that way."

"Me too. Let me get that for you." John nodded and went outside.

A short while later, Bonnie was in her uniform, the one she'd packed instead of wearing. Maybe it was just as well, she thought as she put her wet jeans and sweater into a plastic bag that Sandie had given her.

She glanced at herself in the bathroom mirror. She looked tired and slightly angry. Her hair needed a good brushing, but the brush was in the other suitcase. She wasn't going out for it.

This was as good as it was going to get.

## Chapter Four

Bonnie had never been involved in a murder investigation. She'd been part of several drug stings and investigated out of season hunting incidents and other wildlife related issues. She'd drawn her gun but never fired it except at the range.

Sitting across from Chief Rogers and Officer John Trump made her nervous.

"This is a map of the island," John told her. "You can see the various landmarks. If you could put an X near the spots Harvey and Ray Hoy were killed, that would help the investigation."

She picked up the pencil and made a small X near the old dock and a few hundred feet away to the south where she'd found Harvey and the wolf.

"How much time was involved between each man being shot?" Chief Rogers asked.

"I can only guess about Harvey since I wasn't there

when it happened. I'd say there was about twenty minutes between Ray Hoy being shot and when I found Harvey."

"What about the weapon?" Chief Rogers asked.

"Hoy had a rifle with him. I don't know if that was the weapon that killed Harvey. I'm assuming there was another person on the island. Someone shot Hoy, but I didn't see who."

John looked at the chief. "I could probably get both men to Sevierville."

"I don't want to risk that," Chief Rogers said. "They'll keep until tomorrow. We'll take them over to the ice house. It should be plenty cold to keep them. We're gonna have our hands full here with the storm."

"All right." John nodded. He smiled at Bonnie. "That's enough for now. If we have any other questions, we have your cell phone number."

"You're not trying to get down the mountain tonight, are you?" Chief Rogers asked her. "We have plenty of places to put you up in town. I don't want you to end up in a wreck."

"No, I don't plan to go down the mountain. Thanks." The idea of driving in the snow and ice made her shiver. She'd never liked it when she lived here. She was spared that weather in Alabama. It would take some time to get used to it again.

Sandie gave her a map that they normally gave out for the Sweet Pepper Festival. It looked like a cartoon but showed all the local places she could find a room for the night. "Your best bet is probably the bed and breakfast right across the street," she said. "Even if the place was full, she'll take in stragglers because of the storm."

"Thanks." Bonnie took the map from her. "Any idea

where I could get something to eat?"

"I think the cafe is closed, but Flo always has something. Let's hope this snow has stopped by morning, or we'll all be in a pickle."

Bonnie's cell phone rang. It was Matthew Brown Elk.

"Are you almost done in there?" he asked. "It's been three hours. How many questions can they ask?"

"I'm finished now. How's the wolf?"

"He's sleeping comfortably. I guess you're not going into the valley tonight since the road is blocked. Where are you staying?"

She looked at the cartoon map. "I guess I'm staying at the bed and breakfast across from town hall. Where are you?"

"I was planning on sleeping in my truck. You're welcome to join me."

Bonnie smiled at the invitation. "Why don't you come to the bed and breakfast?"

"I don't think Flo would thank me for bringing your wolf there, and he needs to be kept warm tonight. He can't sleep in the truck by himself."

She felt guilty that he had to sleep in his truck to take care of the wolf she'd saved. "Where are you now?"

"Outside town hall. They're bound to stay open all night—protect and serve, you know. At least they'll have a pot of coffee on and bathrooms. I'm staying where I am."

"All right. Thanks." She put her phone in her pocket. It looked like she was going to be spending the night in his pickup. She wouldn't be able to sleep knowing he was out there because of her.

She'd also grabbed the heavy coat that went with her

uniform. It was like new since she'd only worn it a few times in Alabama. Asking Sandie if she could leave her suitcase there, she draped Matthew's coat over one arm and picked up two cups of coffee before she went out into the storm.

It was easy to see why the roads out of Sweet Pepper were blocked. The storm had gathered intensity and had already blanketed the area with at least a foot of snow. Under that was the ice that had first accumulated. The roads that had been difficult were going to be impassable.

She found Matthew's truck parked along the curb close to town hall. Her wet tennis shoes were freezing in the snow. She hadn't thought to bring any boots with her, other than rain boots. She'd have to shop for a pair as soon as she could. It was December in the Smoky Mountains. There would be snow through March or April. She was going to need some warmer clothes too.

Bonnie tapped on the driver's side window, and Matthew rolled it down.

"Coffee?" she asked as the steam from the hot cup swirled with the snow.

He looked surprised. "Thank you. The bed and breakfast is just over there. Sorry I can't offer to drive you. I don't want to lose this space—close to necessary services."

She didn't answer but hurried around to the passenger side, shoved in his jacket, and hopped up on the seat. "You go on to the bed and breakfast," she said. "I'm the one who brought the wolf. You shouldn't have to suffer for my actions."

"I've spent more nights in this truck than I care to remember. I'll keep watch on the wolf."

"Where is he?" She changed the subject since she knew she wasn't leaving. "How's he doing?"

"He's right here in the back." He turned on the overhead light so she could see the wolf. "He's doing all right for an animal that was shot and burned. He's young. He should recover."

Bonnie peered around the seat. The little wolf was sleeping on her jacket. Matthew had cleaned him up, and his wound was no longer bleeding. She smoothed her hand across his head where he hadn't been injured.

"Thank you." She turned back to face Matthew. "Burned and shot?"

"Yep." He tossed a small bottle to her. "I got the bullet out. I guess he was involved in the gunfight with Ray and Harvey."

She examined the bullet in the plastic bottle, holding it up to the light. "Not a bullet from a rifle. It looks more like a .38."

"That's what I thought too. What the heck was going on out there?"

"I guess we'll have more answers tomorrow once the fire brigade gives its report and the coroner has a look at Ray and Harvey."

He turned off the light and sat back in his seat sipping his coffee. "You better head over to the B and B. I think we might already have more than a foot of snow, and it's not slowing down."

"I'm not leaving." She sat back in her seat and drank some of her coffee. "But you can. I promise to keep an eye on your truck."

"You're kind of stubborn, aren't you?" There was a smile in his voice.

"That's what my parents always said. I like to think

of it as tenacious."

"Not a bad quality for someone in your line of work. How'd you become a federal agent anyway?"

Bonnie watched the snow hitting the wide windshield, grateful for the warmth of the truck—and hoping he had enough gas in the tank to last the night. She was glad he finally accepted that she wasn't leaving, but she wished he would have taken her up on her offer to stay there without him. He seemed to be a nice enough person, but it was still awkward staying in his truck overnight. She supposed she could have moved the wolf to her pickup, but she was exhausted. And the heater in her truck wasn't as good.

Something else on the list, she thought sleepily.

She indulged his curiosity by briefly explaining how she'd decided to become a Wildlife Agent. "I've always loved wild animals. My mother used to complain because I brought rabbits and snakes inside all the time so I could take care of them. It's what I wanted to do as an adult too."

"Why not work for a zoo or an animal refuge?" he asked.

"My father was in law enforcement. I guess I wanted to roll the two together after he died. He was killed during a traffic stop on the highway near Sevierville. I was twelve at the time."

"I'm sorry. My father died when I was young too. Nothing so dramatic. His tractor rolled over him."

"That's terrible too. I'm sorry." She put her cup of coffee in a holder between the seats and yawned. "So what do you do?"

"I still grow Christmas trees in the valley. Same piece of land—but I never take a tractor out by myself."

He paused. "Why did you leave the valley to find your career? Seems like there are plenty of jobs around working with animals. You could've been a part-time cop too."

She snuggled into her jacket. His had been much better since it was bigger, but hers would have to do. "I had to leave. I didn't ever plan on coming back to stay."

"But sometimes things happen," he replied. "I guess you had to come back to be with your mother, huh?"

Bonnie's even breathing and failure to reply told him that she was asleep. He tucked his coat across her, leaned back in his seat, and closed his eyes.

* * *

It was morning when she awakened. For a minute she couldn't figure out where she was. The windows were covered with snow. Her back hurt, and the wolf behind her was crying out.

Matthew was on his knees leaning across the seat. "Swallow some of this, little man. It's guaranteed to make you feel better."

"Is he all right?" Even though her brain felt sluggish, she could still remember the wolf she'd rescued.

"He's in some pain. I made a paste with some herbs for the pain. He takes it pretty well."

"I'm surprised he'd take it from you that way. What's in it?"

"The herbs aren't as important to getting him to swallow it as the bacon flavoring I put in it." He soothed the wolf with a salve on the burned parts of his body.

Bonnie watched him through the sliver of space between his back and her seat. "You're really good at this. I'm surprised you're not a wildlife vet."

"School and I never got along. It's just come to me

so I could help animals when I need to. But I told you, I'm a tree farmer at heart." He sat back in his seat. "My coffee was gone a long time ago. How about yours?"

"Sure. I could use something hot." She moved his jacket toward him. "You might need this."

"It stopped snowing a couple of hours ago." He put on his jacket. "The cold set in after that. They're saying it's a couple of degrees below zero. I'll be right back."

But it wasn't as easy to get out as he'd expected. The snow was higher than the bottom of the door and glazed with ice. He had to lean back in the seat and kick the door open. Snow fell on him from the roof and blew into the truck.

"Don't try that at home." He grinned at her and was gone.

Bonnie checked her phone when he was gone. There were messages from her brother and mother, but she had no service to return the calls. She sighed as she took a closer look at the wolf. The herbs Matthew had given him had taken away the pain, and he was sleeping. He looked so thin and frail. She hoped he'd survive and that she'd be able to reintroduce him to his natural habitat.

When Matthew didn't return right away, she decided to go inside to wash her face and get her own coffee. She felt sure no one was going to be out to steal the truck. There were no footsteps or tire marks in the pristine, white blanket that lay over the town.

Matthew was on his way out as she was going in. He handed her a cup of coffee. "There are donuts too. I didn't have enough hands to grab any and thought you might not want to eat them after they were in my pocket."

She laughed at that. "I've eaten a lot of food that was

in a pocket. Best place to keep it, right?"

He took a donut out of his pocket and took a bite of it. "Still good."

Bonnie went inside and set her coffee down on a table. She saw the pastries next to the coffee pot, but she headed to the bathroom first.

The mirror told her that she'd slept well enough for being in a truck all night. Her face looked better, and she felt better too. She felt the plastic bottle in her pocket that held the .38 slug and decided to turn it over to Chief Rogers right away. It wasn't exactly in the chain of evidence, but it would have to do.

Chief Rogers was talking to Sandie, who had changed clothes during the night and didn't look at all as though she'd spent the night in the office. They both wished her good morning and told her to take as much coffee and donuts as she wanted.

"Thanks. I wanted you to have this. It's possible it could be from the same gun that killed Harvey," she told him as she explained the circumstances she'd come by it. "I didn't realize the wolf had been shot."

"Just as well," Sandie remarked. "They probably would have killed him and removed the bullet. How's he doing? I'd love to see him."

"We wouldn't have killed him," the chief defended. "But we'll see if this bullet matches Harvey's wound. I thought it was a rifle that killed him?"

Bonnie shrugged. "Ray Hoy had a rifle. I was going by that. I guess this means for certain that someone else was out there too."

"Maybe." He shook the bullet in the bottle. "I might have to get a corroborating statement from Brown Elk about removing it from the wolf."

"I don't think he's going anywhere. At least not right now." She grabbed a donut. "Thanks. How's the weather report?"

"It looks like blue skies later this afternoon," Sandie said. "But between now and then isn't going to be a picnic."

As she said it, the lights in the building went off.

"I hate when I'm right." She sighed.

## Chapter Five

Matthew was cleaning the snow from his truck as she went out. There was a thick crust of ice on all the vehicles that had sat out during the night. As soon as he'd finished cleaning his truck, Bonnie borrowed his scraper and cleaned her own. That was another thing to add to the list, since she hadn't used one since she'd left home.

She didn't see any point in starting her vehicle since it had almost bald tires and wasn't going anywhere until the streets were clear. Freezing, she got back in Matthew's truck. He had a CB radio and was talking to someone about plowing the streets.

When he was finished, he explained that Sweet Pepper wouldn't get a county snow plow until at least tomorrow. "We usually get some local folks in to take care of it. The small plows are at least as good as one big one."

"I can move the wolf to my truck now," she said with a smile. "Thanks for your help."

"You know, I was thinking we could really use that Hummer about now. We should put the wolf inside and let Sandie keep an eye on him. We could take my truck over to the ice house and get the keys for it from Harvey's body."

"Can we do that before the autopsy?" She felt faintly wrong about that. It seemed like something they shouldn't do, although she agreed about the Hummer. It could go through the snow and ice like nothing.

"I don't see why not, but if it would make you feel better, we can ask Chief Rogers what he thinks."

"You might have to give him a statement about the bullet. I already gave it to him."

"That's okay. I was expecting it. Let's take the wolf inside."

A generator had already kicked on to supply lights and heat for town hall. John Trump was on the phone with other officers and people who could use their snowplows to dig the town out that day. Sandie was fielding calls from residents about loss of power and people who needed to get out of their homes for one reason or another.

Matthew shook hands with Chief Rogers and told him his plan. The chief thought about it, not responding right away.

"That's fine. You have a federal agent with you. She can keep track of everything. Make sure you have a complete record, Agent Tuttle. I have some evidence bags and a pad of paper. Just don't move him."

Bonnie took it all and put it in the old satchel she'd brought from her truck. She'd collected evidence before but not from a dead man. She guessed it was basically the same procedure.

"I'll want that statement, Brown Elk, as soon as you get back," Chief Rogers said. "The coroner is already gonna want a piece of me for all the discrepancies in the way these deaths have been handled."

"I'm sure he'll understand that no one expected any of this to happen," Matthew said.

The chief grunted. "You don't know Judd Streeter. But we'll deal with that later. If you know anyone with a plow, I'd appreciate if you gave them a call."

"Already on it." Matthew saluted him.

"Why don't you work for me? I could use a man like you."

"That's probably why," he retorted. "We'll be back as soon as we can."

Sandie was already cooing over the wolf that was sleeping in a dog bed and kennel that she'd found somewhere in the building. "He's so precious. Are you going to keep him, Bonnie?"

"No. The idea is to get him well enough and then release him back into the wild," she answered with the stock reply she'd been taught. "He's a wild animal. We don't want to take that away from him."

"I'd take him in a heartbeat if it was me," Sandie said.

"Yeah," Matthew added. "Just keep your fingers away from his face. He should sleep until we get back."

They went back out to his truck. The heat had already dispersed, although the windows were clear enough to drive. He added some gasoline from a metal can in the far back and climbed inside to restart the engine.

Bonnie was glad that the heat came back on. "How far is the ice house? Can your truck get through it?"

"With some help." He nodded to one of the Sweet Pepper Fire Brigade engines that had been outfitted with a plow on the front.

"So where are you off to?" a young man asked from the window of the vehicle without leaving it.

Matthew yelled back over the noise of both engines. "We need to get to the old ice house by the pepper factory. Think you can make it?"

"Are you kidding me? This lady will get you all the way to Sevierville if you want to go that far." The young man nodded at Bonnie. "Who's your friend?"

"Ricky Hutchins," Matthew introduced them. "This is Federal Wildlife Agent, Bonnie Tuttle. She's way too mature for you, and she carries a gun."

"I'm not a kid anymore, Brown Elk. No one is too mature for me. And I like women who carry guns." Ricky waved and smiled at Bonnie. "Nice to meet you. Ignore anything this man tells you."

She laughed and waved back. "Nice to meet you."

They followed in the cleared wake of the large fire truck. There were no other vehicles on the road, but people were out trying to dig their way through the icy snow. The white coating was beautiful on the mountains and trees, making a picturesque image that was right off of a Christmas card.

The toll on the people was always the hardest. Like the tree branches that came down from the weight of the snow, many people would have heart attacks shoveling. There would be wrecks once everyone was out and moving around again. Any severe weather was stressful for humans.

"Will you live with your mother or at the cabin Harvey used that was provided by the state?"

"I'll live with my mother," she said. It hadn't been a hard decision, knowing that her mother needed her. But giving up her independence had been an uncomfortable moment. "After all, it's why I'm back."

He glanced at her. "Not even a twinge of homesickness for the old place?"

"I've missed the mountains and the fir trees." Bonnie smiled. "I've even missed the snow."

"But not the people. I get that. They can be a bunch of nosey, small-town jerks if you let them."

The fire truck slowed to a stop. They hadn't reached the ice house yet. Matthew got out of his truck to see what was wrong when Ricky left the engine. Bonnie followed, curious, and willing to help if they needed it.

One man had ventured out. His car had slid sideways in the road and blocked the way in or out of Sweet Pepper. Old Doc Schultz was still in his flannel pajamas with a hooded parka thrown over them, his feet stuffed into knee-high boots.

"What brings you out so early?" Matthew asked the older man.

"Stupidity. That's what brings me out. That and the town needing a new doctor to tend to the people of Sweet Pepper. We need a clinic or some damned thing so people don't have to drive all the way into Sevierville every time they need stitches. I'm supposed to be retired."

"We appreciate you, Doc," Ricky said. "What's up? Maybe we can get you where you're going."

"Some fool up at the pepper plant cut his hand on one of the machines and is no doubt trying hard to bleed to death before I can get there. You knuckleheads could've had the streets paved by now." Doc stamped his feet in the cold, his breath tuning frosty in the air.

"Climb in my truck," Matthew told him. "We'll let Ricky drive this tank up the hill first. I'll call someone to move your car."

"Sounds like a plan, if that offer comes with a ride home too." Doc shook his head. "I've had that offer way too many times and got stranded places not to throw in that caveat."

"You got it." Matthew nodded. "This is our new Federal Wildlife Agent, Bonnie Tuttle."

Doc's wizened brows knit together. "Tuttle? You must be Rose's girl. I think I delivered you. I hope I remember every baby that ever slid into my hands, but the mind plays tricks on you. Welcome back to Sweet Pepper. Let's quit standing here in the cold and get going."

Matthew called the police about the car after he'd helped Doc get into the warm truck. They were fortunate to be right at the turn to go up the mountain to the pepper processing plant. Ricky skirted between the edge of the road and the car, maneuvering carefully until he made the turn.

"I can't believe that fool didn't fall off the side of the road," Doc Schultz remarked. "He's reckless with that vehicle. I don't know why Chief Griffin lets him drive it."

"He hasn't wrecked it yet," Matthew replied. "I've heard he's handy with the engines too."

Bonnie listened to their conversation as they went up the slippery road that led to the pepper factory. The business, owned by the Carson family, had been there for a hundred years. She remembered taking tours of it when she was in school. Most of the people in the area, including Christmas Tree Valley, worked there. Growing the trees required maintenance but wasn't a full time effort.

Doc Schultz thanked Matthew after he'd helped him out of the truck. "Don't forget my ride home."

"I won't. I'll be back for you as soon as we get this lady the keys for her Hummer."

"I always wanted one of those. Couldn't afford one on what a country doctor makes. Don't take too long."

The large parking lot had been cleared of snow and ice. Salt had been applied to make sure it didn't refreeze. Matthew made a wide circle in the lot and started back down the steep hill. He'd only gone about a hundred feet before he made a sharp turn onto a gravel road. The ice house was at the end of that road.

Bonnie considered that Doc Schultz only thought Rick Hutchins was a bad driver because he hadn't been in the truck that long with her companion. She kept one hand on the armrest and one on the cup holder between them.

"Nervous?" he asked. "Don't worry. You'll get your snow legs under you after a while. You must've driven here in the snow before. You never forget how to do it."

"It wasn't something I was happy about then, and I'm not looking forward to it now," she replied. "But you're right—I'll get used to it."

He pulled the truck to a stop in front of the old ice house. "They say they used this to store ice before it was available everywhere, including your freezer. Now they only use it for hunting sometimes when someone needs to store a kill. Do you want me to come in with you?"

"No. I'm fine. I'm glad you could bring me up here. I hope they can come get these bodies later today." She took the key from him and opened the door, conscious of him watching her. It was only the aftermath of a horrific day yesterday and sleeping in the truck last night. Everything felt so new and strange. The rest of it could've waited a day or two until she got a chance to acclimate.

A single bulb hung down from a wire in the ceiling. The switch to turn it on was beside the door. She was glad there was a light even though it wasn't very strong and moved as she walked by it.

There were two long, wood tables that each looked a hundred years old. The rickety legs barely supported the six-foot flat surfaces. Only one table had something on it. She guessed it was both bodies stacked together. The medical examiner really was going to have a field day with this.

But when she pulled back the tarp, there was only one body—Ray Hoy. She put the tarp back on him and took a step back to examine the rest of the room. Her mind was telling her that Harvey had to be in here, but she couldn't see him. It didn't make any sense for anyone to put him on the floor or under the other table. She took out her cell phone and switched it to flashlight mode to add some strength to the dim overhead light.

The room was only about eight by ten. There were only the two tables. The walls were bare except for some string and wires. There was no sign of Harvey.

The door opened, and she put her head up, startled, knocking the top of it on the bottom of the table.

"Something wrong in here?" Matthew asked. "I was getting worried. Having trouble getting the keys from

Harvey?"

"No. He's not here. Someone must have moved him."

## Chapter Six

He followed the same routine she did searching the small building. He crawled across the dirty floor, which she hadn't been willing to do, but the result was the same.

"Where did he go?" he asked.

"I have no idea." Bonnie shivered. The ice house was colder than it was outside. "Let's get back in the truck and call Chief Rogers. Maybe someone came for the body."

But Chief Rogers knew nothing about it. "Was the lock still on the door?"

"I opened it with the key you gave us," she told him. "It hadn't been cut or forced."

"Ray Hoy is still in there," Matthew said as they used the phone in speaker mode. "But no sign of Harvey—not even the blanket I put around him."

"That doesn't make any sense," Chief Rogers said.

"I just spoke to Judd Streeter. He says the roads are too bad to come until tomorrow. I know he didn't come for him."

"Who else has access to the key?" Bonnie asked.

"Just me, usually," the chief responded. "No one else uses it anymore. I gave you the only copy of it, as far as I know."

Matthew shrugged but remained silent as he stared at the ice house through his window.

"I'll send John out there," Chief Rogers said. "Don't worry. We'll get to the bottom of this."

"Do you want us to wait until he gets here?" Bonnie wasn't sure what was going on but didn't want anything happening to Ray's body too.

"I'd appreciate that. I don't want to have to look for two corpses. Thanks."

She put her phone in her pocket when the chief finished. "I guess we'll wait. Sorry to get you into this. I'm sure you have better things to do."

"Not really. Not until some of this snow has melted. We're in the middle of the tree season right now. But I don't expect many people to be out today looking for a Christmas tree."

He went on to talk about how the business had changed since he was a kid. Matthew ran his tree farm with his brother, Tom. "My mom has retired from it. She watches my son for me while I'm working."

"Oh. You have a son? How old is he?"

"He just turned five this year. His name is Peter."

"Does your wife work in town?"

"I don't know." He glanced away as he answered. "We haven't seen her since Peter was born."

"I'm sorry. It's good you could be there for him."

She wished she wouldn't have asked.

"Where else would I be? Mara didn't want Peter, but I persuaded her not to get rid of him. As soon as he was born, she was gone. We weren't married. It was an accident. Not a pleasant one for her."

That hit a little close to Bonnie's heart, and she stopped asking questions. It was hard to sit around with someone and not talk about their lives.

As if he could sense the truth about why she'd left Christmas Tree Valley, he asked, "What about you? Any kids? Married? Why did you leave the valley?"

She wished she could get out of the truck and walk away, but the situation didn't allow for that. "No kids. No husband. I was young and looking for something else, I guess."

"Something you found in Alabama that you couldn't find here," he guessed. "Until now. And still, only the most dire circumstances bring you back."

"I visit every year. It's not like I haven't seen my family in ten years.

"Yeah. I get that."

The sun played through the tree tops above them as the sky slowly turned blue. The ice on the trees looked like a diamond glaze that sparkled and shone with prisms of light. It wasn't long before the heavy snow on the branches above them started falling on top of the truck.

"It never takes long," Matthew finally said. They'd been quiet for a while, each lost in their own thoughts. "Most of this will be gone by tonight."

She laughed. "Just in time for everything to freeze again when the sun goes down. I haven't been gone that long."

John Trump pulled up in a jeep. Just as Matthew got out to talk to him, Bonnie got a call from her brother.

"I'm going to miss my plane if you don't get here soon," Eric said in an irritated tone.

"You told me it was okay to leave Mom alone for a while each day while I'm working," she answered. "Get on your plane. I'll be there as soon as I can. Some things came up when I got to Sweet Pepper, worse things than the snow and ice."

"Look, this is a great opportunity for me. You've already wasted your life. I shouldn't have to waste mine too."

This was the way their conversations always sounded. Eric resented her for leaving the valley but had still chosen to stay, even before their mother got sick. Bonnie felt guilty that he'd always been there for her mother and put up with his annoying tone.

"I'm not saying you should waste your life. I'm stuck here right now. I'll be there as soon as I can."

His end of the phone went dead. She knew the conversation was over. Matthew had opened the driver's side door as she'd finished speaking, so both he and John Trump had heard the last of her heated words to her brother.

"We found some tracks going from the back of the ice house," Matthew said without mentioning her phone call. "John wants me to help him follow them in case it's the person who took Harvey."

"If you have somewhere you need to be," John said, "take my jeep. We can trade cars later. I'll come back with him."

Bonnie stepped out of the truck. "I'll go with you. I found Harvey, and I owe it to him. I'm sure the Wildlife

Agency would want me out there."

"Okay." John smiled at her. "Let's go."

She was grateful to them for not asking any questions about her conversation. Eric's job would keep—he was leaving two weeks early anyway. Bonnie was sorry she wasn't wearing boots, but she did have her service revolver and her ID. Her brother was just going to have to understand that this was part of her job.

"You can see where someone got through this rotted wall," Matthew said as they circled around the ice house. "You couldn't see it as well inside because of the lighting. I'm guessing they got Harvey out this way."

Bonnie crouched close to the crumbling concrete. "There's something here—maybe some skin and clothing." She pointed to the find.

"There was some snow on the ground already when this happened," John said. "But at least another foot has been added."

"But under that top layer of ice, the snow is still soft," Matthew added. "If we're careful, we should be able to follow where they went. Once we reach the trees over there, they act like a snow break, keeping the snow from falling under them. That's where we'll see the best tracks."

He was right. It appeared whoever had taken Harvey's body half carried, half dragged it away from the ice house. There were more incidents of pieces of clothing that snagged on trees and even a single shoe that had been left behind.

As they got into the thick, pine forest, the snow was thin, even spotty in places. It was simple to follow the trail as Harvey's dragging feet showed them the way.

John got ahead and pointed out the boots that led

the way before the drag marks. "Looks like a big fella. Look how deep these prints go into the ground, even though it's frozen on top."

Matthew nodded. "About a size twelve, I'd say. No deep marks like hiking boots. These are more like city boots or biker boots."

They both compared the boots they wore to the marks.

"Not cowboy boots either." John grinned at Matthew's boots. "Not pointy enough."

"Not work boots with steel toes either," he said to John. "The toe would go down further. Do you want us to compare yours too, Bonnie?"

They all looked at her ruined tennis shoes. She wished she could hide them under the pants leg. "That's okay. I'll have to get some boots. I don't think those marks look like something I could make."

"Let's keep going," Matthew suggested. "We've still got another mile or so to get down the mountain. That's the only place someone could get in a car or truck and transport the body."

John nodded in agreement, and they continued down the slope.

Bonnie was starving by two p.m. but didn't mention it. John brought out a candy bar, and they split it three ways. Normally she was better prepared for being outside for an extended length of time. With no water to drink, they ate some of the clean snow as they walked by it.

The air in the pine forest was crisp and clear, heavy with the scent of the big trees they passed. No animals crossed their path—probably still wherever they could find to stay warm. They had better sense than to be out in the cold or caught in their burrows without food. They could wait out the snow.

Feet hurting in her wet shoes, Bonnie was glad when they finally reached the main road that ran out of Sweet Pepper. Doc Schultz's car had been towed, and the warm sun had left only patches of snow and ice on the road. Of course the vehicle that had transported whoever had stolen Harvey's body was long gone, but John and Matthew found deep tire prints in the semi-frozen mud along the side of the road.

"I think we should be able to make a cast from this," John said, using his cell phone to take pictures of the marks. "I'll get someone out here right away."

"And we need a ride," Matthew said.

"What about Doc Schultz?" Bonnie asked.

"He probably intimidated someone into taking him home by now," Matthew answered. "But we can check to make sure. Thanks for reminding me."

John was on the phone alerting Chief Rogers to their findings and requesting transport back to the ice house. "I'll stay here until we can get castings of these. Brown Elk and Agent Tuttle need a ride as soon as possible."

He'd just finished saying the words when a bright red Jeep Cherokee with the Sweet Pepper Fire Brigade emblem slowed to a stop beside them.

"Never mind, Chief. I can get them back up there. I still need that casting set though."

Stella Griffin rolled down her window and smiled at them. The strong breeze from the mountain swung her red ponytail around. "What's going on? Good to see you again, Bonnie."

"You too, Chief Griffin," Bonnie replied. "We could really use a ride up the mountain to the ice house."

"Brown Elk?" Stella responded. "Are you up for that?"

He glanced inside the Cherokee and shuddered as he shook his head, his long, brown hair flying. "I'd rather walk up there, Chief. Thanks anyway. I'll just give Bonnie my keys, and she can come back to get me."

"Is something wrong?" Bonnie wondered, looking at them. They sounded as though they'd had this conversation before.

John started laughing. "It's the ghost of the old fire chief. Brown Elk says he can see him and it creeps him out. Isn't that right?"

"I can see him," Matthew agreed. "He doesn't creep me out, whatever that means. It's just not good to hang around with spirits. No offense, Chief Griffin."

"None taken," she replied. "Give her your keys, and we'll bring the pickup back to you."

Bonnie got the keys and went around to the passenger side. She started to open the door when John called out, "Not there. You'd have to sit on top of him."

Stella and John both laughed at that. Matthew didn't find it amusing. Bonnie wasn't sure how to take it. She got in the front seat next to Stella and pulled on her seatbelt.

"I guess he moved to the back seat," she said wondering if this was an ongoing joke between them. Matthew was scowling.

"I'm glad you find it amusing," he said to John and Stella. "You don't know the power of the spirits for good and evil. It may not seem like it, but it's better to be safe and away from them than under the ground with them."

"Okay. Sorry," John said. "We'll see you in a few minutes."

Stella's Cherokee took the mountain and the occasional patches of ice that remained in the shadows as though they weren't there.

Bonnie felt like she had to ask so she understood what was going on with these people she'd be seeing on a regular basis.

"I don't talk about it much. People in Sweet Pepper would have regular conversations with me every day about Eric Gamlyn if I did." She kept her eyes on the road. "When I first got here, they told me the old cabin was haunted. I laughed until I found out it really is haunted by the first fire chief."

"I remember. That's the cabin up on Firehouse Road. We used to go up there and try to do magic spells and other stupid things," Bonnie said. "That's the ghost? My mother said she used to date him in high school. That's the only reason we thought he was real. How strange is that?"

"Very strange," Stella smiled. "But not as strange as knowing he's in the back seat right now. Do a parlor trick for us, Eric. Hold up my jacket. I don't think Bonnie can see you."

Obligingly, her heavy jacket went straight up in the air and from side to side before falling back to the seat.

"Wow." Bonnie's eyes grew wide. She was impressed but not afraid. "That's really something. Does he do anything you tell him?"

"He says he's not a zombie." Stella laughed. "He definitely doesn't do anything I ask. But he's a great cook, which comes in handy before the Sweet Pepper Festival, and he's not a bad companion."

"And he travels around with you?" Bonnie couldn't stop herself from glancing into the back seat but couldn't see anyone. "I thought ghosts lived in haunted houses."

"He was confined to the cabin for a while, but now he can leave as long as someone has his old badge with them." She looked in the rearview mirror. "She's not going to tell anyone, Eric. You're just paranoid."

Stella didn't say anything else, but she appeared to be listening. Bonnie couldn't hear Eric Gamlyn either.

"That's right," Stella finally said as if she was in the middle of a conversation. "Eric introduced me to your mother at the Pepper Queen's coronation party a while back. I take it the two were close, but Eric went away, and she married someone else."

"Yes. Her first husband, Wendel Harcourt. He was my brother's father. She remarried after he died and had me."

"He wants to know how Rose is doing."

"She's got Alzheimer's, but it's in the early stages right now. She's doing okay. Does he ever visit her?" Bonnie thought it might be a good idea to know if the ghost came and went at the house. It could save her from thinking she was crazy if things started moving by themselves.

"Not unless I'm there. I mostly carry his badge with me."

"Well, tell him I'm very pleased to meet him. He's the first ghost I've ever met."

"He's laughing," Stella said. "He says you can talk to him yourself. He can see and hear you just fine. And you remind him a lot of your mother."

A chill went down Bonnie's spine, and she shivered. Coming home was turning out to be a whole different thing from when she left.

## Chapter Seven

Stella dropped her at the ice house, waving as she left once she had the truck started. Bonnie followed her back down the mountain.

She didn't feel overwhelmed by realizing there was a ghost in the back seat of the Cherokee. On the other hand, she'd been raised in these mountains with plenty of scary tales of ghosts and other supernatural creatures. She wondered if the old mill to the north of Sweet Pepper was still haunted or if the ghost on Second Street who lost her head was still looking for it.

Another officer in a Sweet Pepper squad car had joined John and Matthew on the side of the road. Stella had parked her distinctive red vehicle along the edge too and was watching them mix and pour the solution into the tire marks to make casts of them.

Bonnie parked on the road too—it was beginning to look like a stopover for a parade. When she got out,

Matthew was ready to go. He grabbed the keys from her and headed back immediately to the truck.

She ran after him. "Hey, wait a minute. I need a ride back to town hall."

"Come on then." His steps didn't falter. "I don't like standing around with ghosts either. You can bet when you see Chief Griffin that she has Eric Gamlyn with her."

Bonnie got in the truck and slammed the door closed. "You really don't like ghosts, do you?"

"Like I said—they're bad news. I don't care how friendly he is. I wouldn't want to be around Casper. It's just that simple. The dead are supposed to stay dead."

"Okay. Sorry."

"So now what?" He took a deep breath and seemed to be more normal when he spoke. "It's going to take a while to locate Harvey unless someone drops him off for us to find. Maybe you should have Chief Rogers get someone in to make a new set of keys for the Hummer."

"We might have to do that," she agreed. "But I have a lot to do before that. I'll probably just drive my truck for a while until things have a chance to settle down. Thanks for your help."

"Glad to be there." He smiled as they reached town hall again. "I think I'm going to run over to the cafe for some real breakfast. Come join me if you get a chance."

"I will. Thank you."

They parted at the curb with Bonnie going inside to talk with Chief Rogers. She watched Matthew as he headed down the sidewalk. He was a big man, with a powerful chest and wide shoulders. People moved out of his way as he walked. But he seemed to know most of them and stopped to talk with a few.

Chief Rogers was waiting for her. "Anything yet on

Harvey's body? I hate to tell his wife and kids that we lost him."

"Not yet. They were just letting the casting set when I came back." She swallowed hard and glanced at him. "I'll tell them, Chief. I was with him. He was kind of my partner. I'll take care of it."

He nodded. "All right. I'm glad to have you here, Agent Tuttle."

"Thanks, Chief." She shook his hand. "I still might need some help with the Hummer if we can't find Harvey or the keys have gone missing."

"Not a problem. If I know Harvey, he left a spare set in his office. You just have to be able to get down the mountain to Christmas Tree Valley. Good luck with that before tomorrow."

"I guess I'll get there as soon as I can. I'd appreciate it if you let me know if you hear anything about Harvey."

He nodded and went into his office.

Sandie was glad to give up custody of the young wolf. "I didn't have any trouble with him. What are you gonna do with him?"

"I hope to get him well again and release him into the wild," Bonnie told her. "Thanks for keeping an eye on him."

"No problem. Tell your mother I said hello. I hope to see you again soon when it doesn't have anything to do with murder."

Bonnie carefully lifted the wolf that was still nestled in her jacket. Lucky for her it wasn't an expensive jacket because she probably wouldn't be able to get it clean when it was over.

"Easy boy," she said as she opened the door to her

truck. Most of the ice and snow had melted off of it. She had to move some of her things—she'd brought everything she owned with her—to make the place for the wolf on the front seat. He growled a little then went back to sleep with his tail curled around him.

She wanted to take a look at the road that led down to the valley. Maybe enough people had gone down that way that she could get down there too. She got in and tried to start the truck, but when the engine wouldn't turn over, she closed her eyes and took a deep breath.

"That doesn't sound too good," Matthew said. "Pop the hood, and I'll take a look at it. It might just not be used to the weather."

Bonnie rolled down the window. "Thanks. I thought you were going to be at the cafe?"

"I forgot to give you my secret concoction for your wolf. How's he doing?"

"About the same." She took the bottle that looked like it had Grey Poupon mustard in it. "This goes on him, not in him, right?"

"Right. I don't want to continue sedating him. It will make it harder for him to heal. He'll get a little friskier, but that's the way he should be. Make sure you wear gloves when you handle him."

She stifled a frown at his comment. Just who was the Wildlife Agent here? "I appreciate it. Let me try the truck again while you're here."

He nodded after opening the hood. She turned the key and nothing happened. He did something under the hood that she couldn't see and told her to try it again. The engine just wasn't starting.

After a long day yesterday and the early hike through the snow this morning, Bonnie was ready to scream. Her phone rang—her brother again. She ignored it, since nothing had changed.

"Leave the truck here for now," Matthew advised through her open window. "I'll put some chains on my truck, and we'll get down the mountain. I know you've got stuff to do. No point in sitting around up here."

It appeared to be the only answer she could find. She knew Eric was antsy to get on the plane and start his new life. She needed to get the wolf settled before the sedative Matthew had given him wore off. Without the keys for the Hummer, this was her best chance to get to the valley.

"I know I seem to be saying this a lot, but thanks." She smiled at him as she got out of the truck. "I'd like to take a few things with me, if you don't mind. I can get someone to take care of the truck tomorrow and get everything home after that."

"I'm happy to help." He grinned. "And this way if I ever get on the wrong side of the Wildlife Agency, you'll owe me."

"You're right," she agreed. "Let me get my stuff."

While Matthew put the chains on his tires, Bonnie grabbed three essential bags that held toiletries and some clothes she'd need. She asked Sandie if it was okay if she left her truck where it was for now. Sandie told her it would be fine.

After putting her bags into Matthew's truck, Bonnie carefully grabbed the wolf and got him comfortable in the back seat.

"We're right back here again, huh, boy?" She stroked his head. "Trust me, we'll get past this. You're gonna be okay."

Once everything was set, Bonnie called her brother

and told him she was leaving Sweet Pepper. He had nothing to say but a bunch of snarky remarks that she ignored.

"You're smiling," Matthew observed as he got behind the wheel. "That must be a good sign. If you can still smile after everything you've been through since yesterday, things are looking up."

She fastened her seatbelt and hoped the steep road to the valley was in decent shape. "It wasn't how I'd envisioned coming home for good, but I'm sure it will all work out."

He started the truck. "What are you going to name the wolf?"

"I'm not naming him anything. It's not like he's a pet I'm going to keep."

"Yeah but he's going to be part of your life for a few weeks. He needs a name. How are you going to call him if he doesn't have a name?"

They had reached Christmas Tree Valley Road. A dozen signs showed pictures of cars and trucks at steep angles, some of them bent where they'd been hit by an errant fender. Bonnie could see the snow covered valley before her, and the snow covered road in front of her that dropped with a thirty percent grade.

"All right," Matthew said. "Hang on to your hat."

Because there were so many trees on the ridge above the road, very little morning sunlight reached the road. Afternoon sunlight would melt the snow and ice, leaving puddles that would freeze during the long night. People who made it into the valley today would have a hard time getting out again tomorrow.

Bonnie kept one hand on the door, but even though she was scared, she had to admire the serene, winter beauty of her home. Christmas Tree Valley didn't have a big population—three hundred and sixty two the last time she checked. There were a few churches, their steeples still sparkling with white crystals, and the general store that doubled as a post office. The rest were houses and buildings. Interspersed with the houses and storage buildings were Douglas fir and blue spruce trees that reached for the sky.

She could pick out the tree farms because the trees grew in a more orderly fashion. Hundreds of acres were devoted to growing the best trees in the world. A large, wood-and-brass plaque at the general store had the names engraved of every family that had grown a Christmas tree for the White House. There were many names celebrated there. It was the brass ring that every farmer reached for.

"Did anyone have a tree for the White House this year?" she asked Matthew.

"Nope. Not for the last few years. It doesn't seem to hurt business any—not like this snow and ice will. But people still like thinking about it. My brother and I have been getting a tree ready for next year. Our family has never grown one that went to Washington."

"My grandfather grew one," she said, her nose almost pressed against the frosty window to look out at the colorful scene stretched before her all the way to the mountains behind. "I think that was in 1950."

He laughed. "Don't toy with me. Like you said, you haven't been gone that long. Everyone who lives here can tell you exactly what date, who was in office, and how tall the tree was. Go on. Spill it."

"You're right. It's like learning multiplication here, isn't it? Our tree was twenty-five feet, three inches, blue spruce, and the president was Truman."

"I knew it. You were trying to spare my feelings, weren't you?"

"You're either one way or another about the trees," she remembered. "Either you gloat or you're modest about it. My mother taught me not to gloat."

"Lucky it was you with the tree and not me. My dad taught me to gloat. If we have a winning tree next year, I'll be gloating."

Bonnie laughed at him. "You just don't seem like the type."

One of the tires hit a slick patch on the road that looked as though it had snowed only a few minutes before. The wheel slid to the side of the road, too close to the edge that only had a flimsy looking guard rail.

She caught her breath, but he got the truck back on track. Her hand ached from holding the door handle so tightly.

"Sorry about that." He glanced at her. "You're white as a sheet. I guess you really don't like driving in the snow. You're gonna have to get over it, you know? You'll have a heart attack or something."

"Don't look at me," she instructed in a panicked voice. "Keep your eyes on the road." She reached over and put her hand on his on the steering wheel. "And remember the ten and two positions? You should have your hands at those places for optimum control of the vehicle."

"Yes, ma'am. Don't worry. You're safe with me."

She looked at her hand where he'd covered it with one of his. "Onehanded now? I don't feel very safe."

He laughed at her and put both his hands on the wheel again. "You know how many times I've come down this road drunk as a skunk? Not for a long time now, but when I was in high school, I didn't think anything of it."

The road turned sharply in almost a U-turn that required the truck to rumble to a stop to get around the edge of a large rock that protruded on one side. Bonnie closed her eyes and didn't open them until she heard the chains jingling as they started down the last part of the road.

"See? Nothing to it," he boasted. "I drove one of the semis that takes the trees out of the valley for a while. Talk about a wild ride. I'm glad to leave that to someone else now."

The last part of the road wasn't as steep and smoothed out as it came down in the valley. A large sign that said, "Welcome to Christmas Tree Valley, Home of the Best Christmas Trees in the World," had been newly painted since she'd been there over the summer. Two big trees were on either side of it, both decorated with lights and large ornaments.

As they were coming into the small main area, Bonnie got excited as she always did when she came home to see her family. No matter how long she'd been in Alabama, this would always be the place she came back to. She'd never really thought about living here again, but it looked like that was her future. Except for driving during the winter, it didn't seem so bad.

## Chapter Eight

Bonnie's family tree farm was nearly one hundred acres of carefully pruned and cared-for blue spruce. A smattering of Douglas firs edged the property—wild trees but never cut down. The two large blue spruce guarded both sides of the driveway, only garnished with snow and icicles, but they were breathtaking.

"Where do you live, Matthew?" she asked as they started up the drive. Someone had been out with a plow or snow blower already. Very little snow was on the road or the drive. Bonnie remembered that everyone took turns clearing the road since the county never sent plows this far out from Sevierville.

"I'm about a mile that way." He pointed back the other way. "You could see my place from the road coming down. We put on a bright red roof last year, and it says 'Merry Christmas from Brown Elk Farms.' We get customers before they even get off the road."

Bonnie had noticed the red roof that was especially bright in the snow. The Merry Christmas part had been obscured by the white stuff, but it still made a powerful statement.

"We might have to steal that idea from you," she joked.

"Go ahead. I borrowed it from someone else anyway."

Eric had seen them coming from the house and stepped outside. He smiled when he saw Bonnie get out of the truck and walked out to greet her with a big hug. Their mother was right behind him with tears and kisses when she saw her daughter.

"Thanks for bringing her down the mountain." Eric shook hands with Matthew. "She might not have made it down until spring with the way she feels about driving in the snow."

Bonnie watched the two men together. Eric was tall and strongly built, muscular from years of working on the tree farm. He was blond and blue eyed and had just turned fifty. Her mother had been blond too, with blue eyes. Her hair was white now.

She didn't remember Eric's father. He'd died before she was born. Her father had married her mother when Rose was in her late thirties. Bonnie had been born a short time later. That made Bonnie and her brother almost twenty years apart and like a whole other family.

Matthew was taller than Eric and much darker. The two made an interesting picture, standing together as they spoke. It was not surprising that he and Eric knew one another. Everyone knew everyone else in Christmas Tree Valley. No doubt she'd bumped into Matthew earlier in life without remembering him when they met again.

"Come inside, and let's warm up with some hot cider," Rose invited him.

"I'd love to, but Peter is with Tom. I know they've been wondering when I'm getting back. Raincheck?"

"Always." Rose smiled at him.

"I'll see you later, Bonnie," Matthew said. "It's been a pleasure. Don't forget the pup."

As he was heading back to his truck, Eric and Rose asked, "Pup?" in unison.

Bonnie didn't answer. There was time enough for that later. She ran to get her things, handing them off to Eric so she could bring the wolf inside.

He glanced at the wolf pup, a frown between his eyes. "A wolf pup? Where did it come from?"

"I'll explain over cider after I've had a chance to change clothes and get my feet warm. I hope I don't have frostbite on my toes. I'm exhausted, starving, and freezing. Everything else can wait a while."

Rose had already made lunch. Bonnie went to her old room and changed out of her cold, wet clothes. She put on some sweatpants and a sweater. Her toes were fine when she put on double pairs of wool socks and let out a sigh of relief. At least that part of getting home was over.

With a hearty pot pie on the table, they sat down for lunch, and Bonnie told them about everything that had happened since she'd gotten to Sweet Pepper.

"That's terrible," her mother said. "Harvey's family is only two farms down. He was such a young man and had those two children, Abigail and Gerald. Who would want to kill him?"

"Maybe it was an accident," Eric suggested. "Maybe

someone was hunting on the island. Is that what happened to the wolf pup?"

"I don't know yet," Bonnie said, opening a hot corn muffin and slathering butter on it. "Nothing is getting done because of the weather."

"Except for criminal activity," Rose reminded her. "Sweet Pepper isn't big enough for those kinds of things to go on."

"I met someone interesting while I was working," Bonnie told her. "Remember when you used to tell me about Eric Gamlyn, the old Sweet Pepper fire chief?"

Rose appeared confused for a moment, but her frown passed, and her blue eyes lit up. "Of course. We probably would have been married if he hadn't left town so suddenly. He wasn't the fire chief then, and his family didn't have much money. He came to see me the night before he left and asked me to wait for him. I might have too, if it wouldn't have been your father, Eric. He swept me off my feet. You were born the next year."

"Probably just as well," her brother said. "At least we had a good insurance business while my father was alive to subsidize the tree farm."

"Well, anyway." Bonnie tried to bring the conversation back. "They say the old fire chief haunts the fire brigade, and the new chief, Stella Griffin, says she can see and talk to the ghost of the old chief."

Eric, always pragmatic, made a spitting sound like ice hitting the window. "There's no such thing as ghosts. She was just pulling your leg—you know, making fun of the new person."

"No," Rose said. "I believe it. If anyone could come back from the dead, it would be Eric Gamlyn. He was so strong and always did what he said he was going to do.

I heard he made his fortune digging for gold in the Yukon or some such. He was quite the character."

"It seems odd that you named our Eric after him." Bonnie smiled as she finished eating.

"Oh, that." Rose waved her hand. "It was a family name from Wendel's side. It had nothing to do with the other Eric."

After all of his complaining, Eric's plane had been grounded until the next day. Bonnie was glad it happened. She needed a truck to fulfill her promise to Chief Rogers and notify Harvey's family. She wasn't happy about going out again, but she had no choice. His name was being withheld from the media until his next of kin were told.

She got dressed, and Eric offered to go with her. It gave them a chance to talk about their mother and everything Bonnie needed to know about the farm.

"Mom's holding her own right now," he said as he drove to the Shelton place. "She has some bad days, but she takes her meds. She's hanging in there, fighting as hard as she can."

"You left all her information somewhere for me, right?"

"That and everything else—what I've done with the trees this year and planting instructions for next year. I hire two people that help out. If you can't do that on your salary, let me know, and I'll help you. It's too big a job for one person with a day job."

"How have sales been this year?"

"Brisk. Starting the sleigh ride into the fields was a good idea, but it added a horse on the payroll. I think people really like it. It would be nice if we had some other things going on here besides the general store and the Christmas House. A few people are talking about adding some lights to Main Street and getting visitors to come at night for them. I don't see that happening without a hotel down here so people don't have to leave. No one wants to come down the mountain in the dark."

"I understand that." She glanced up at the mountain she'd come down with Matthew.

"Anyway, we're members of the co-op. I already told them that you're taking my place on the board. You'll have to help make those decisions. Any questions or problems, you can call me. I know you won't because you're so stubborn. But I'm there if you need me."

They touched on Eric's recent divorce after ten years of marriage.

"Julie moved back to Knoxville. I got to see her and Annie right before the storm hit." Annie was his three-year-old daughter.

Bonnie squeezed his arm. "I'm sorry. I know it's hard. That's really why you're leaving, isn't it? You've been offered promotions before and never took them because it meant not being here."

"I just decided it was time for you to come home." He smiled at her. "What about that man you liked in Alabama—the cook with the white gator? Why didn't he come with you?"

"The relationship just never got that far." She thought about Saul Chase, but there wasn't enough between them for her to mourn. She'd enjoyed his company, but he was a free spirit. He didn't seem interested in a commitment. "I would've enjoyed him being here on the long, cold nights. Mom would like him. He's a great cook."

He patted her shoulder. "You'll find someone if you

can let go of the past."

"I don't want to talk about that. There's the Shelton place." She pointed, glancing at the address on her cell phone. "Don't pass it."

"Forget I said that about the past, little sister. You just need to stop being so bossy. No man wants a woman to tell him what to do."

"Never mind." She took a deep breath as he parked the truck. "I have to do this."

In a clean, dry, brown Wildlife Agent uniform, Bonnie went up to the door, leaving Eric in the truck. She squared her shoulders as she knocked. Children's Christmas decorations were on the windows, and Mr. and Mrs. Santa Claus were in matching rockers on the porch.

Mrs. Shelton opened the door. A younger man and woman stood behind her. They both had the same pale blue eyes as Harvey—his kids. Children screeched in the background, with the sound of little feet running through the house.

"Oh my God," Mrs. Shelton said, tears beginning to stream down her face. "I knew something was wrong. When Harvey didn't call, I knew something bad had happened."

Bonnie cleared her throat. "I'm sorry, ma'am. Agent Shelton has been shot and killed."

Mrs. Shelton's legs gave out. Her son and daughter supported her and helped her into the living room. Bonnie followed them, closing the door behind her. The Shelton women held each other and cried, while Gerald stood stoically behind them, staring at a blank spot on the wall.

Bonnie stood quietly but didn't know what to do

with her hands, finally settling on clasping them in front of her. She had only made one other death notification in her career, and that had only been as a second party with a sheriff. It wasn't an easy or pleasant thing to do. Somehow it seemed worse at this time of year.

"Would you like some coffee?" Abigail asked after several minutes, tears still in her eyes.

"Yes, please," Bonnie said, corners of her mouth turned down. She sat in the cozy room with them. A fire was crackling in the hearth that was hung with red stockings.

"Tell me what happened," Mrs. Shelton said in a voice devoid of emotion.

Bonnie explained the situation and what had happened as far as she knew. She left out the part about not being able to find Harvey's body. It didn't seem important or appropriate for the grieving family.

Mrs. Shelton sobbed as her son put his arm around her. He looked just like his father.

"I'm sorry, but I need to ask you a few questions," Bonnie said as Abigail brought in cups of coffee for all of them on a large Christmas tray.

"That's all right," Gerald replied. "We want to help."

"Do you know if Agent Shelton had any enemies?" Bonnie took out a scrap of paper and had to borrow a pen. She wasn't prepared for this.

"Harvey didn't have an enemy in the world," his wife said. "As far as I know, everyone thought the world of him."

Her children agreed with her. Bonnie hadn't expected anything different from them.

"Why was Harvey retiring so early?" Maybe it

didn't have anything to do with his death, but she'd wondered from the beginning.

"No specific reason," Mrs. Shelton said as she wiped her tears away. "He just came home one day and said he thought it was time."

"He wasn't sick? Decided the job was too much for him?"

"No. We talked about doing some traveling. His brother lives out west."

So nothing there either. "Has he mentioned any problems that have to do with the job? What was the last thing he did?"

Mrs. Shelton shook her head. "I can't remember right now. I wish I'd paid more attention. I'm sorry, Agent Tuttle. But I'm so glad you're here to take his place. He loved the area, and I know he'd want someone like you to take care of it."

She started sobbing again. Bonnie knew it was time to leave. She didn't have any printed cards yet but wrote her cell phone number on a piece of paper and left it for Harvey's family in case they thought of anything else.

"What about my father's body?" Gerald asked as he walked her to the door.

"The coroner will have it for a while. Someone will be in touch with you when you can make arrangements. Do you know if your father had an extra set of keys for the office and the Hummer?"

"Sure. Let me get those for you." He studied her face. "My mother might need some time to get out of here, Agent Tuttle. I know this house belongs to the Wildlife Agency."

"Don't worry about it. I'm living with my mother anyway. Tell her she can take all the time she needs."

Bonnie was glad to walk out of the small cottage with the Hummer's spare keys. She wondered where his office was located. She could probably look that up without asking anyone.

"How'd it go?" Eric asked when she got in his truck.

"About like you'd expect." She closed the door on the frigid air and let out a breath she didn't realize she'd been holding. "Let's get back. There's nothing more I can do today. Tomorrow was supposed to be my first day working. I think that's what I'm shooting for now."

But it wasn't easy to get Harvey's death off her mind. Bonnie spent the evening playing scrabble with her mother and brother. She went to bed early and found the wolf pup wide awake. He growled at her as she put on her gloves and started smoothing the salve Matthew had given her on him. He calmed down right away, as though he knew she was trying to help him.

She looked into his intelligent, brown eyes as his gaze followed her every move. "You're awfully tame for a wild pup, aren't you?"

He opened his mouth and let out a weak howling sound.

"Well, that was something." She stroked his head. "Just don't get too attached. I have to let you go in the wild as soon as I can. I can't believe Matthew thought you needed a name. That's kind of crazy, isn't it?"

The wolf howled again but settled down in her jacket.

"I'm not kidding," she told him. "When you're better, you're out of here. You'll see."

## Chapter Nine

The next morning dawned bright and clear. The sun glistened on the snow as it began to melt it in earnest. The roads were full of puddles, and snow dripped into icicles that hung from the roof. It was a picturesque scene throughout the valley.

Eric's flight was leaving early. His truck was staying—good thing, since Bonnie's truck was mostly dead and she didn't want to drive the Hummer when she wasn't working. The gas alone would kill her. She was only allowed a certain amount every month.

She and her brother continued talking about the tree farm and upcoming events that she'd have to take over. Groups of people came randomly to cut their own trees and take them home, but the real money was in special parties that included food and games. She would have to be home for those, working them into her schedule. That was barring emergencies, of course. Bonnie hoped everything would fit together.

"I love you, sis." Eric gave her a big hug and kiss before he left. "If anything at all gets messed up, give me a call."

"I will." Bonnie hugged him tightly. This might be the closest she and her brother had ever been. With such a wide age gap between them, they weren't close when she was a child. It was too bad that his leaving had brought them together.

Driving his pickup back from Sevierville, Bonnie thought again about Harvey. She also had to decide how she was going to get Eric's truck and hers home, as well as bringing the Hummer down the mountain.

She stopped on the side of the road as she saw a group of older children with sticks poking at an animal. At first she thought it was a dog but soon realized it was a red fox. Not only could they be hurt by the fox, the fox could be hurt too.

The sign near the abandoned convenient store said she was in Frog Pond, another community mostly served by Sweet Pepper fire and police. Her own jurisdiction was much broader, including several counties in the area. Not that jurisdiction would have stopped her from dealing with the fox problem.

"Hey." She approached the group. "What's going on? You know that fox isn't tame. He could take on all of you and come up the winner. He wouldn't hesitate to bite you, and he could have rabies."

The two smaller children dropped their sticks and ran away. But the older boys gazed at her arrogantly.

"What's it to you?" one of them asked.

She pulled back the lapel on her brown jacket so they could see her badge on her uniform. "I'm the new

Federal Wildlife Agent. You know what that means?"

The second boy threw down his stick but didn't leave. "It means you protect animals."

"It also means I protect people *from* animals. You should both go on home and let me deal with the fox."

"Yeah, well, my dad says the only good fox is a dead fox."

A pickup in worse shape than Bonnie's pulled to the side of the road with them. An older man got out, hitched up his pants, and came toward them. He was short with a heavy pelt of yellowing white hair on his head.

"Morning, ma'am." He nodded to her. "Is there a problem here? These boys giving you a hard time?"

"Nothing I can't handle." She put out her hand to him, hoping he wasn't related to one of the boys. This could take a lot longer if she had to argue with him too. "I'm Agent Bonnie Tuttle, Wildlife. And you are?"

"I'm Walt Fenway. I used to be police chief in Sweet Pepper. I'm retired now, but I keep my eyes open. I didn't know there was a new Wildlife Agent. Did Harvey retire?"

"No, sir." She glanced at the two boys who were watching them closely. "We should talk about this later. Right now, I need them to leave this fox alone before one of them gets hurt."

Walt peered around her at the exhausted fox, who was lying still on the gravel at the edge of the road. "He's a beauty. You mean to take him in for protection?"

"I'll have to take a look at him. If he's not seriously injured, I'll just get him out of here."

"You boys head home," he told the pair. "And next time you see a wild animal, you leave it alone."

"Yes, sir," the second boy said. "We were just having some fun."

But the first boy wasn't finished yet. "I can do what I want. My dad says foxes kill chickens. What difference does it make if I kill him?"

Before Walt could speak, Bonnie had removed the handcuffs from her belt and put his wrists in them.

"Hey! What do you think you're doing?" The boy was starting to panic. "You're not the sheriff."

"You're right," she told him. "I'm a federal official. I could arrest the sheriff if I wanted to. I have jurisdiction over this whole area. I could call the FBI to get you and take you to a federal prison. You wouldn't be back here mouthing off and asking for a wild animal to bite you for twenty years."

He glanced at Walt. "Is that true?"

"You know it, son. Better take her seriously."

The boy stared at Bonnie, scared now. "I won't bother him again. We were only having some fun. Give me another chance." His voice cracked. "I'm just a kid."

She glared at him for a moment, conscious of the other kids watching too. "I'll give you one more chance, but you have to attend some wildlife classes." She took off his handcuffs. "Your friends too. I want each of your names, addresses, and phone numbers. I'll let you know when classes start."

The kids gave out their information easily after that. They disappeared into the snowy woods.

"That's a good way to take care of it." Walt eyed her warily. "Now what happened to my friend Harvey Shelton?"

Bonnie gave him the whole story except for Harvey's body going missing. She knew how the area was. The snow had slowed the gossip, but it wouldn't be long before everyone knew that he was dead. She hoped they'd find Harvey's body before everyone knew about that too.

"That's a crying shame." Walt bowed his head. "Harvey was a good man. I can't imagine who would've wanted him dead."

She thought this was a good opportunity to ask someone outside the family about her predecessor. "Have you noticed anything unusual about him in the past few weeks?"

"No, not really—though I thought it was strange for him to decide to retire out of the blue. I still didn't really believe he'd do it until I met you."

"Did he say anything about it? His wife told me he wasn't in bad health and didn't think he was having any trouble with the job."

"Nothing I heard." He pondered the question. "I just thought it was strange, and he didn't want to talk about it. I guess that was strange in itself and one reason I thought he was just yanking my chain. Harvey liked to talk."

"Any other ideas?" she asked.

"Would you consider telling me what kind of gun killed him?"

"A .38 caliber. I have the slug that was taken out of a wolf pup who was shot at the same time."

He nodded. "So it was personal, huh? I mean, he wasn't shot at the same time as Ray Hoy. And to go through him into the pup means it was close range. I'd take a guess that it was someone he riled over enforcing wildlife regulations. That's the best I can do."

"Anyone in particular come to mind?" she pressed.

"As a matter of fact, I believe the last man I remember him mentioning was Vince Stookey. They got into a dust up about a month ago when Harvey caught him poaching a doe out of season. Maybe you should give him a call."

Vince Stookey's name had come up with Matthew too as Ray Hoy's associate. It seemed she would have to talk to the man once she could find him. Bonnie thanked him and had to write her phone number on another piece of paper to give him. She really needed to get her business cards.

The small red fox was sitting up when she looked back at him. He didn't seem injured—maybe only playing dead so the boys would leave him alone. He seemed healthy, a good size, and no foaming at the mouth. His eyes were calm on her as he watched her move.

"He seems okay to me," Walt observed.

"That's what I thought." She stared back at the fox. "I think you better get home now. The road is no place for a fox to be. It's going to get cold again later. Go find your den."

With a small yip, the fox turned and trotted off into the woods.

Walt hooted and slapped his thigh. "I believe you talked him into it! You've got a way with wild animals, don't you?"

Bonnie smiled. "They just want some respect. Thanks for your help, Walt. I'm sure I'll see you around."

They parted on the road in Frog Pond, each going their own way. Bonnie still had the problem with getting the vehicles back to her place. She decided to stop in at town hall and ask for help. She was sure they didn't want the Hummer out at the lake any more than she did.

On the way back to Sweet Pepper, she pulled in at the fire brigade station at the end of Firehouse Road. The station had been rebuilt since she'd lived here before. Funny how many things she didn't notice during her summer visits. She glanced up at the road that eventually led to the old cabin where Eric Gamlyn had once lived.

Many times on a dare, she'd gone up that road as a teenager. The old cabin was a favorite drinking and making out spot for everyone she knew. Not inside the cabin—no one would do that. She'd heard a few unusual noises when she'd knocked on the door as part of the dare, but she'd always gotten away from there quickly, not wanting to find out if there really was a ghost.

She went inside the station, thinking she'd like to invite Stella out for a drink to thank her for her help. The crew was cleaning up the building and washing the two large firetrucks. A few men called out to her. She recognized them from the island fire.

Ricky Hutchins jumped down from one of the trucks. "Hey, Bonnie. Great to see you. I'm glad you got out okay. Everyone—this is the new Wildlife Agent, Bonnie Tuttle. She's from Christmas Tree Valley. Say hi and be nice. You never know when she might be the only thing standing between you and an angry mama bear."

Bonnie laughed at that. "If that happens, you better have a candy bar to throw at her. I don't want to pick up anyone's pieces."

The men, and two women, laughed and went back to work after welcoming her. Tagger came out of the small room with a door that was labeled

Communications. The big man—Rufus—who was on the radio yesterday was there too, though he was busy with something in the communications room. The only person who wasn't there was Stella.

"Yeah," Tagger said scratching his head. "She had some big confab with Chief Rogers this morning. Probably something to do with the fire. But I'll tell her you stopped by. It's nice to see you again."

"Thanks," Bonnie said, turning to go. She glanced on the wall in the dining area and saw several old pictures of the first fire brigade. The names of the men were clearly labeled. There was also a newspaper clipping that was framed. The article was about finding the person who had killed Chief Gamlyn, with a picture of him when he was alive—it looked like his official portrait as fire chief.

She gasped as she got up close to it. He looked just like her brother. It was a resemblance that was unmistakable. At least one big question came into her mind.

"That's the old chief." Tagger saw her interest and rushed to help. "He was a great man, saved my life more than once. Sorry the chief has him with her. I'm sure he'd like to meet you."

"Are you trying to scare her off?" Ricky asked. "Don't listen to him, Bonnie. Everyone says there's a ghost, but I've never seen him."

"Actually, I met him yesterday when Chief Griffin gave me a ride up to the old ice house."

"Really?" Allen Wise asked. "What were you doing up there?"

"Don't be stupid." Tagger glanced at him. "Where else were they going to keep the two dead men since they couldn't get them to the coroner?"

"That makes sense," Ricky agreed. "So you saw Chief Gamlyn?"

"No," Bonnie replied. "But Chief Griffin introduced us."

She promised business cards to all of them in case they needed to call her about any kind of wildlife issue. They all invited her out for drinks at Beau's Tavern. Bonnie left, glad that she stopped, even though Stella hadn't been there.

Snow was falling in wet blotches from the trees and powerlines as she drove into downtown Sweet Pepper. There were very few vehicles on the road despite the clear skies and warm temperatures. Everyone knew that would change later and were trying to dig out before it happened. The only place open was the cafe and town hall. Two yellow tickets were on her truck, requests to move the vehicle for the bigger snow plows to come through.

Bonnie parked Eric's truck beside her own and took the tickets inside with her. She wasn't sure what to do with her truck. Maybe she'd have it towed somewhere that it could be repaired. She had plenty of vehicles to get her where she needed to go. She could bring her truck home when it was in better shape.

Sandie offered her coffee as she went inside. "We've got fresh cinnamon rolls from the cafe too. How's that little wolf doing? He was as cute as button."

"He's doing fine. I think he'll make a full recovery."

Bonnie got a cup of coffee and started to grab a cinnamon roll—the whole place smelled wonderful because of them. The door to Chief Rogers' office opened, and he and Stella came out.

"Just the person I wanted to see," he said. "Stella, if you have another few minutes, could you come into the conference room with us?"

## Chapter Ten

"I appreciate you doing that notification, Bonnie," he said when they were seated at the big table. "I hate to ask, but did you talk to them about anything they might have noticed different about Harvey in the last few weeks?"

"I did. And I also asked if he'd had any trouble at work or anyone he'd had trouble with recently."

He grinned. "Now that's what I'm talking about. Go on. What did they say?"

Bonnie explained that his wife and children didn't have much to say. "She didn't understand exactly why Harvey was giving up his job. I've heard that from more than one person and wondered myself."

Chief Rogers wrote down what she said. "It's a good question. He wasn't old enough to retire, and if his wife didn't even know, I'm not sure how we'll find out."

"I'm going to the office later," Bonnie volunteered.

"I'll look through his papers and see what I can find."

"Sounds good," he said. "Stella, anything your firefighters saw at the island could be helpful. I'd appreciate it if you'd ask them some questions."

She nodded. "You got it."

"Thanks." He shuffled through his papers. "Judd Streeter will be here soon. He can get what he can from Ray Hoy, but there's still nothing on Harvey's body. I hate to tell him that, but that's where we are."

"What about the tire print?" Stella asked. "Anything from that yet?"

Chief Rogers squinted at his notes. "We've got the tire info—seventeen-inch Michelin. Has to be a good-sized vehicle. John is running with that, but there are a lot of big vehicles in this area that could have been out during the storm."

"Isn't there a tire registry or something?" Stella asked.

"There is," Bonnie replied. "But there's nothing stopping someone from putting that tire on any vehicle."

"That's right," Chief Rogers agreed. "Once we get to the identification of the vehicle, that will come in handy. Right now it doesn't do us a damned bit of good. So whatever you two can come up with, I'd appreciate the help. It's bad enough to have Harvey's death hanging over us. It's a lot worse that we lost his body."

"I didn't mention that to Mrs. Shelton," Bonnie added.

"Good idea. Maybe we won't have to," Chief Rogers said. "I guess that's about all. Let's hopes this freeze tonight isn't too bad. We need to get moving on this."

As they got to their feet, Bonnie asked about help getting either the Hummer or her brother's truck back to the valley. "And if either of you know the name of a good mechanic who can tow my old pickup to his shop, that would be great."

Stella laughed. "That's a lot of vehicles for one person. I'll be glad to drive one of them down for you, and you can give me a ride back here. Ricky Hutchens is the only mechanic I know. He works on our trucks, but he works full time for Ben Carson too, so I'm not sure if he'd have time to take a look at it. But I'd be happy to ask him."

"Never mind all that," Chief Rogers said. "That boy's got his hands full. I'll give Max Morrison a call, and he'll come for it. He has a friend who works on the vehicles he brings in."

"Thanks, Chief Rogers." Bonnie took a card from him for the tow service.

He shook his head. "Don. Let's see if we can get you settled in here before you need to do anything else. How's your mother doing?"

A chilly breeze rustled the blinds at the windows and made the papers on the table flutter. Bonnie glanced around the room, wondering if that was Eric Gamlyn's reaction to the question. She also noticed that neither of the two chiefs seemed to notice. It seemed to her that Chief Rogers must be used to it and Chief Griffin expected it.

The next moment, Stella's cell phone and radio went off.

"I'm sorry, Bonnie," she said. "Someone was using a barbecue grill in their house to heat, and now we've got a structure fire. If you can't find anyone else before we get done, I'll still be glad to go with you."

Chief Rogers also had a call from one of his officers.

He left her in the conference room with his cell phone on his ear.

Oh well. She wandered out of the room, not knowing who else to ask for help. She could call to have her pickup taken care of, but that still left her with a vehicle she couldn't drive down the mountain by herself.

"Looks like you've been busy." Matthew hailed her from the coffee table with a cup in one hand and a cinnamon roll in the other.

"It's already been that kind of morning." She smiled as a thought occurred to her. "I was wondering if you'd be willing to drive one of my vehicles home for me. I got the keys for the Hummer from Harvey's family. I just can't drive that and my brother's truck down the mountain at the same time."

"I get that." He nodded as he swallowed. "I'll be glad to help—if I can drive the Hummer."

"That wouldn't work, since the Wildlife Agency won't let anyone drive their vehicles except their agents. My brother's truck is pretty new." She tried to entice him into driving it.

"Okay. But you're buying lunch, right?"

"Right," she agreed with a smile as she handed him Eric's keys. "Thanks. I have to call about a tow truck, and then I'm ready to go."

Max Morrison said he'd be over to get her truck as soon as he finished a call to pick up a stranded driver. She thanked him and walked out of town hall with Matthew.

"Any news about the missing body?" he asked.

"Not yet. We're all trying to figure out why Harvey was killed right now. Chief Rogers says the coroner will be up here today. That's going to be embarrassing."

"I guess so, even though there were extenuating circumstances." He drove slowly through the empty streets with Bonnie on the passenger side.

The elegant gingerbread houses on Main Street were beautiful, draped in their white coats. Icicles glistened off the edges of the roofs, and children took advantage of their day out of school to build snowmen and forts. Bonnie and Matthew laughed at a snowball fight between a dozen children as they went by.

"Lucky for you, we didn't live in the valley when you were a kid," he said. "I make a mean snowball."

"Not better than mine. I sent many young boys home crying."

He smiled at her in a way that made her feel awkward. "I'll bet you did."

Luckily they were turning down the gravel drive to the landing where she'd left the Hummer. It was covered in snow that hadn't melted quickly, since it was beneath heavy tree branches. They got out and had to scrape the snow and ice from the vehicle for several minutes.

Bonnie finally had enough space cleared on the driver's side to open the door. She pulled it hard to break the icy seal that had been created overnight. As she did, Harvey's body dropped at her feet.

Surprised by it, she jumped back and lost her footing, falling on her butt as she stared at the dead man.

Matthew came around to her side quickly. "Are you okay?"

"Yes. I guess we found Harvey before the coroner got here." She sighed.

* * *

Chief Rogers asked them to stay at the scene. Judd

Streeter had just arrived. They were coming out to them shortly.

Matthew crouched at the side of the Hummer without disturbing the body. "Look here. The same size twelve we saw at the ice house today. And I'll bet we find those big tire tracks here too."

"But why?" Bonnie wondered. "Why steal his body and put it back here?"

He looked up at her. "Kids' pranks?"

"That would be a pretty weird prank." She studied Harvey's body without touching it. "Look at his clothes. I think someone went through his pockets."

"Maybe just to get the key," he suggested.

"It's not just that," she said. "The rest of him looks mussed too. And the buttons on his shirt aren't fastened correctly. I think someone might have undressed him as they looked for something they didn't find in his pockets." She took several pictures with her cell phone.

"That's possible. If so, it probably had something to do with his death."

The siren from Chief Rogers' car was getting closer.

"It had to be something really small if they thought he had it on him."

He shrugged. "It could be anything."

She agreed as the coroner—who reminded her more of Santa than someone who cut apart dead bodies—jumped out of the car. Chief Rogers followed him more slowly. Another Sweet Pepper police car rolled in after them.

"Oh my God!" Judd Streeter yelled as he approached Bonnie and Matthew. "What have you done? This isn't a crime scene, it's a disaster. Didn't anyone teach you how to preserve the scene?"

Chief Rogers came quickly to handle the problem. "Sorry. I hadn't had time to fill him in yet when you called. Judd, this is our new Federal Wildlife Agent, Bonnie Tuttle. And you know Brown Elk. I told you Harvey was killed on the island yesterday. I didn't tell you that we moved him to the ice house until you could get here. Someone took his body last night, and I guess they left it here."

The round coroner seemed only slightly mollified by his words. "This is going to be impossible, Don. I'll do the best I can, but three locations that we know of? No telling where else they took him."

He didn't apologize but immediately started to work looking for evidence on Harvey's uniform and person. Bonnie and Matthew backed away.

Chief Rogers stood with them. "Don't worry about it," he said. "He'll figure it out. Good work, you two. At least Jean Shelton never has to know what happened to her husband after he died. I can take statements from you later, if you like."

But Matthew wanted him to see the familiar tire and boot marks. "I think the same person brought him here that took him out of the ice house."

Bonnie mentioned Harvey's clothes and showed Chief Rogers her pictures. Before she was done, the coroner was looking over his shoulder.

"He was moved so much, his clothes might not mean anything," Judd said.

"But his shirt buttons were redone," she pointed out. "Why would anyone bother with that?"

"You see everything out here, Agent Tuttle," he answered. "I'll let Chief Rogers know of my findings as soon as I can. But don't expect too much."

Chief Rogers nodded and thanked him. "You two can go. This is gonna be a while. Sorry, Bonnie. I know you wanted to get the Hummer back to your place. I'll let you know when the investigation is complete."

"Thanks." What else could she say? She knew the protocol that was employed when a body was found. She wished they could have observed it at the island.

"I suppose you want to drive." Matthew tossed her the keys as they walked back to her brother's truck. "You still owe me lunch. The cafe is open."

She checked her watch. It was slightly after noon. "I should check on my mother, and my brother had someone coming for a tree later today. Lunch at my house?"

"Sounds good."

**Chapter Eleven**

Bonnie dropped Matthew off at his truck, and he followed her down the mountain. The road had improved even more as the sun warmed the day. The pavement wasn't exactly dry, but it wasn't too bad. She was less nervous today about it than she had been yesterday.

Matthew pulled to the side of her truck in the drive. There was already a truck parked there that Bonnie didn't recognize. She got out and looked around. It was kind of creepy knowing that Harvey had been killed. It made her scan the area intensely, even though she doubted that the person who'd killed him had it in for all Wildlife Agents—still a strange feeling.

But the man in the pickup got out with a big smile on his face, and she knew that he was looking for a Christmas tree.

"Need some help with this?" Matthew asked

quietly. "You might be rusty after so many years."

She shook her head. "I think I can manage."

It wasn't something you ever forgot when you were from the valley. How many times had she stood outside in the cold with her grandfather and her father as they walked someone through the trees to find the one they wanted?

"I'm looking for a tree about seven or eight feet," Rev. James from Pigeon Forge said. "I want it to go all the way up. We've got a lovely star for the top." His cheeks were red from walking and the cold. He'd taken some chances coming out there to get the tree today.

"I think we've got what you're looking for," Bonnie told him as they walked toward the bigger blue spruce trees. The trees started at about five feet and went up to ten or twelve feet. They didn't sell many that big, but it happened sometimes.

He stopped as he looked straight up one impressive tree. "Oh yes, this is beautiful! Can I get someone to wrap it and help me put it in the truck?"

"Of course." She smiled. "Do you want to cut it yourself?"

"No. No," he denied. "I don't want to ruin it."

"All right." She got the small chainsaw from the shed where they kept the equipment. "I'll take care of it, and of course we can wrap it for you."

"Thank you. Everyone is going to be so excited when they see it."

Rev. James was twenty dollars short of what she was supposed to ask for the tree, but she gave it to him anyway. The netting machine spun a web around it. She and Matthew helped him load it on his truck and waved as he drove away.

"You're never gonna make any money at this," Matthew told her. "You have to get the money upfront, not after you cut the tree."

"You do it your way. I'll do it mine. But thanks for the help." She smiled. "I really do owe you lunch now."

"I'll say. Maybe dinner too!"

Another older pickup truck came into the drive. Bonnie hoped it wasn't someone else wanting a tree—it was nearly two p.m., and she was starving. Her mother had asked when they were coming in for lunch an hour ago.

But it wasn't someone looking for a tree. It was a tall, dark man who resembled Matthew too much not to be his brother. He was heavier and sporting a small potbelly. He wore his black hair long and free of any restraint. He had a young boy with him—it had to be Peter, Matthew's son.

"So this is where you are," Thomas Brown Elk greeted his brother with a sly smile. "I knew it had to be special for you to miss lunch. Aren't you going to introduce me?"

"Yes," Matthew said. "I was hiding here. How did you find me?"

"I found you," Peter replied. "We were sledding down here, and I saw your truck. Why were you hiding?"

"I wasn't really hiding." Matthew lifted his son and hugged him. "You know today was Uncle Thomas's day to make lunch. I just didn't want to eat his cooking."

Peter laughed. "I know. The meatballs were terrible."

They all laughed at the face he made. Matthew introduced Bonnie to his older brother and son. Rose came out on the porch, wrapped in a heavy shawl, and called them all in for something to eat.

"I have to go to Pigeon Forge for a part for our wrapper," Thomas explained to his brother. "I didn't want to take Peter with me in case it gets late. We know everything will freeze again, and I might not make it back down the mountain."

Matthew nodded and thanked his brother. "I'll see you later. Take care."

"Nice to meet you," Thomas said. "It's good to have you home again. I'm sure your mother is happy to have you back."

Bonnie thanked him and waved as he left. "Come inside. I don't know about you, but I'm freezing."

They went in the house together. Rose was putting lunch out on the table. Steam was rising from the cheese, sausage, and potato casserole she'd made.

"I have a whole room full of toys you can take a look at," she smiled as she told Peter.

"Aren't you going to eat?" Bonnie asked.

"I ate an hour ago," Rose replied. "I can't wait all day for you to come in. You're as bad as your father. I wonder when he'll be home."

Bonnie took off her coat. "He's not coming home, Mom. Remember?"

Rose's smiling eyes blanked for an instant. Then she was right back to showing Peter Eric's old toys as she helped him remove his jacket.

Matthew removed his heavy coat. "That food smells good."

"Thank you. Don't forget to wash up before you eat." Rose reminded him. "You too, Bonnie."

Bonnie washed her hands and then poured them

each a cup of coffee. Eric had told her that her mother sometimes forgot that her father was dead. Rose wasn't in bad shape and was just at the beginning of Alzheimer's. She was stable for now. Still, it was hard not to think ahead to when it would be worse.

"Your mother is a kind woman," Matthew said after he'd returned from washing his hands in the bathroom. "We were all sad to hear about her diagnosis. I hope you'll count on me and Thomas if you need any help."

"Thanks." Bonnie smiled. She wasn't surprised to learn that he was familiar with their house—no one had to show him where to find the bathroom. No doubt her mother had showed Peter Eric's old toys many times. The boy was very polite not to say so.

"Moving into a small, tight-knit place like Christmas Tree Valley can be hard," he remarked as he sat at the table. "Rose made it easier for us—your father too."

She put some of the casserole on both plates and handed one to him. Her father had been dead ten years. It had been a hard time to come back for his funeral and leave again. Her mother had asked her to stay, but Bonnie just couldn't. It was too soon.

"You must've sneaked in under the cover of night for his funeral," Matthew said. "We were there, but I don't remember seeing you. I think I would've remembered."

She smiled back at him. "I had to get back to work pretty quickly. I stayed as long as I could."

He sipped his coffee. "Why did you leave and stay away so long? Your family has always seemed to be very close."

She knew he'd been there for a while and had heard the gossip. Everyone in Christmas Tree Valley knew everything about the people who lived there.

"I'm sure you've heard, and I don't want to talk about it." She started eating as an excuse not to speak.

"Okay." He shrugged. "But you might feel better if you talk about it."

Peter came running in with a model airplane. "Can I keep it, Dad? Miss Rose said I could if you said it was okay."

"Sure. But you have to leave some of Eric's toys here."

"I just want this one thing to go with my collection," Peter explained.

"And what was it last time you were here?"

"I'll tell her you said it was okay." The boy grinned and ran back toward Eric's bedroom.

Bonnie rapidly changed the subject from her past to Harvey's death. "I don't understand why anyone would take his body and then leave it in the Hummer."

"People do strange things sometimes. Maybe the coroner taking a look will help."

"I hope you're right. This isn't a great way to start a new job."

"I'm sure Harvey was glad you were here," he said. "And you'll figure out what happened."

"Maybe." She stared at him across the table. "Wildlife Agents don't spend a lot of time tracking down murder suspects. I'm sure Chief Rogers will be a lot more help."

"One thing I already know about you, Bonnie." Matthew pointed at her with his fork. "You don't give up easy. You'll be that way with Harvey's killer too. Just be careful. You don't want to end up dead like him."

She took their empty plates to the sink. "You've only

known me a day. I don't think you will know much about me."

"I can see into people's souls," he announced as though it was something ordinary. "You have a very good soul. That's why you connect with animals so well."

"If you're talking about the wolf, he was hurt and stunned. I'm sure he won't be such a pushover today."

Matthew got up from the table and thanked her for lunch. "I have to get that recipe from your mom. It was delicious. Why don't we go check on your wolf? Have you named him yet?"

"He's not going to be here long enough to have a name."

He chuckled. "I have a feeling you're wrong about him. He might be attached to you now. If he is, he won't ever leave you. Maybe you could call him something obvious like small wolf or dark wolf. I could look up those names in Cherokee. They might sound better."

Bonnie led the way to the laundry room. "And I know something about you, Matthew Brown Elk—you're a nag."

He denied it as she opened the door. The wolf was sitting in the middle of the room. His eyes were clear and sharp, focusing immediately on her.

"How did he get out of the kennel?" Bonnie asked. She would never have left it unlocked.

"Don't ask me. I don't live here. I think he was waiting for you."

She carefully moved toward the kennel and put on her gloves. "It's going to be hard getting him back inside."

As soon as she opened the kennel door, the wolf

trotted in without hesitation.

"And you've never noticed that you have a way of making animals understand you?"

Bonnie closed the door and carefully latched it. She wiggled the latch to be sure it was secure. "I'm not Dr. Doolittle, if that's what you're saying."

"Dr. who?"

"Never mind." She crouched close to the kennel and studied the wolf as he curled up in her jacket again. "He's just clever. He knew what to do when I opened the door. Wolves are much smarter than people give them credit for." She put a few pieces of chicken from the kitchen in the kennel for him. "I guess I'll need some dog food."

"Get a big bag," he advised with a smile. "That *wahya* is never going to leave you."

Bonnie ignored his predictions as she watched the wolf eat. She could tell his mouth was sore, as he chewed every bite slowly and carefully. "You are a sweetheart," she told him. "But wolves don't belong with humans. You have your whole life in front of you."

Peter came running in to remind his father that they were going to miss a favorite show of his on TV. He and Matthew were getting ready to leave after saying goodbye to Rose.

"If you need anything, let me know," he said to Bonnie. "People in the valley have to stick together, right, Peter?"

"That's right, Dad." His smile showed one missing tooth in front.

Bonnie thanked him. She and Rose waved to them as they left.

"What are you going to do with that wolf?" Rose

asked as she closed the front door.

"Reintegrate him into the wild once he's well," Bonnie answered. She didn't tell her mother that the wolf had gotten out of the kennel. She didn't want to worry her, and she was sure the latch was fastened this time. "I need to run over to Harvey's office. I shouldn't be gone long. Will you be okay?"

"I'll be fine. You have work. I can take care of myself."

"All right. My phone number is programed into your cell phone. Call me if you need me."

"Of course. And don't forget that school from Knoxville is supposed to be here to get their trees this afternoon. It's on the calendar."

"I won't forget." Bonnie looked at her mother. "You could come with me over to the office. I'm just taking a look at it."

"No, I have my knitting. I'm way behind on my Christmas projects. Go on. I'll be here when you get back."

"Okay." Bonnie put on her jacket and gloves. "Be back soon."

It wasn't easy leaving her mother knowing she was sick, and yet Eric had told her not to hover over her. Rose needed to do things by herself too. She hoped there would be some middle ground that she'd find given enough time.

Could Rose have let the wolf pup out? Bonnie would have to pick up a lock for the kennel, just to make sure.

Eric's truck cut through the remaining snow and ice going past the 'downtown' area of Christmas Tree Valley. It wasn't much—some houses, the general store, a place that rented and sold snowmobiles. That was it. If people needed more than that, they left the valley. On nice days, that was fine. When the weather got bad, they had to hope they had enough supplies to wait until the road was clear.

As she turned the truck on to the gravel road that led to the Wildlife office, Bonnie's phone rang. It was Chief Rogers with an update on Harvey's case.

"Did you hear anything from the family about Harvey purchasing an expensive beach house in Hilton Head, South Carolina? We found a real estate transaction in the glove box of the Hummer."

"No, but I didn't ask them about it either. Would you like me to?"

"Sure, since you're out there anyway."

"How expensive are we talking?" Bonnie navigated the rutted drive with one hand on the wheel, despite the snow. Maybe she would actually get used to it. "Harvey would've been receiving his pension you know."

"Think he had a million in there?"

She shook her head and then remembered he couldn't see her. "I don't think so. Are you sure about this?"

"I've got the receipt, and I spoke with the real estate agent. Harvey purchased the place during the same trip he took to Alabama to recruit you. I guess this was a side project."

"Okay. I'll check on it. Thanks."

She'd reached the front of the old log cabin. It wasn't much—barely room-sized, unless it was bigger on the inside. The roof and front porch both sagged under the weight of the snow. She hoped it was safe to go inside.

But there were things she needed to find. Agents kept reports on cases and animals in the area. She needed to have those, and Harvey had already confessed to not adding to a computer as he should have. If she didn't get them now, she might not have another chance, by the looks of things.

She locked the truck after she got out and went carefully up the stairs that also seemed about to collapse. This gift from the state of Tennessee left a lot to be desired.

Bonnie touched the door, and it opened. The key was still in her hand. A sound caught her attention from inside, but before she could push open the door the rest of the way, a man came running out, shoving her roughly to the porch floor.

## Chapter Twelve

She didn't recognize him, but he was holding a stack of files that she might need. Before he could make it down the stairs, she grabbed his foot and pulled hard. He stumbled and dropped the files. His boot came off in her hand.

He swore and started to reach for either the boot or the files but changed his mind and turned to flee. Bonnie pulled her gun and held it steadily on him, even though she was still on her butt in the snow.

"Stay right there," she said. "I've never shot a man, but there's always a first time."

"All right." He sat on the step and held up his hands. "Don't shoot me. I haven't done anything wrong. I just wanted a look at those files."

Bonnie got up and brushed the snow from her clothes. As she approached the man, a huge stag beside a fir tree close to where she'd left the truck caught her attention. It looked just like the one she'd seen on her way into town the other day. He just seemed to be watching her with intense eyes. As soon as she started moving around, he nodded his huge head and went back through the snow.

"Wish I had my gun," the man on the stairs said with awe in his voice. "I've never seen one that big."

"And that's your first response to it?" She cuffed his hands behind his back. "I think you have a lot more to worry about than killing that deer. So what were you doing in there?"

"Just taking a look at Harvey's old files," he repeated. "I was gonna put them back."

"You know that Harvey and I are federal agents, right?" she asked. "That makes this breaking and entering and theft a felony."

"I wasn't stealing," he argued. "I was borrowing. And the door was already open."

"What's your name?"

"Vince Stookey. I'm from Sweet Pepper."

Finally, *the* Vince Stookey she kept hearing so much about. She glanced around the yard that was empty except for her truck. "How'd you get here?"

"A friend dropped me off." He glanced up at her. "You don't need to arrest him too. He didn't know what I was going to do."

"Don't tell me what I need to do." She looked at the boot in her hand. Size thirteen. "What were you looking for?"

"Nothing, really." His eyes shifted away from her. "I was just curious."

Bonnie bent and picked up the files, glancing through them. It looked as though all the reports involved the creeks that flowed through the valley. One of them was a detailed map of the Little Pigeon River.

"Curious about what?" He didn't respond, and she nudged him with her boot. "What were you curious about?"

"I wanted to know if the story was true."

"Don't make me ask you to continue after every few words. Tell me why you were in there."

He rolled his head around and chafed at the cuffs she'd put on him. "I wanted to know if he really found a big ruby or not. Okay? That was it."

She frowned and looked at the maps again. "A big ruby? What are you talking about?"

"I'm not telling you another thing. I want a lawyer."

No matter what she said after that, he wouldn't speak. Eventually she locked him in the back of the pickup, after allowing him to put on his boot, and got as much information as she could carry from inside the office. It looked like all the files Harvey had made. Everything else was just a radio, a chair, and an old desk, mostly empty except a drawer full of junk. The only usable thing in it was a padlock with the key in it—perfect for the kennel. She stuck it in her coat pocket. There was no power in the office. She didn't know if that was because of the weather or if it was always that way.

Finally she got back in the truck and left the valley to drop him off with the Sweet Pepper police. She told Chief Rogers what he'd said and waited to hear what he thought.

"A big ruby?" He rocked forward in his chair. "We've got some mines around here for the tourists, but nobody is salting anything like that with something valuable. He might not even know what a ruby is. I'll talk to him. Thanks for bringing him in."

"I haven't spoken with Harvey's family again, but a big ruby could explain how Harvey could afford a million-dollar beach house."

"True." He frowned. "Harvey's clothes were messed up, like someone was looking for something."

"I know. Could they have been looking for a big ruby?"

"That doesn't seem possible, but I guess you never know. Keep me in the loop with Harvey's family," he said. "I'll see what I can find out from here. It seems to me that it would've made some headlines if a Wildlife Agent found and sold an expensive gemstone."

"Okay. Thanks. I'll talk to you later."

Bonnie met Stella at the door. She was with Ricky Hutchins and another woman Bonnie hadn't met. She was wearing heavy clothes and a Sweet Pepper Fire Brigade sweatshirt.

"We were just going to give you a call." Stella introduced her second in command, Petey Stanze. "We're looking for a Christmas tree for the fire station. Think you could help us out with that?"

"I think so. I was just headed back that way." Bonnie shook hands with Petey, who seemed too delicate to make it as a firefighter, much less second in command. "You can follow me, if you like."

Stella decided to ride down the mountain with Bonnie, leaving Petey and Ricky to bring her Jeep Cherokee down.

A breeze rustled through the files on the dash—a few minutes after the doors were closed.

"You have the ghost with you?" she asked Stella.

"Most of the time. I don't let him go on dates with

me for obvious reasons." She grinned. "He's always telling me I should settle down with someone and get married. But he hates every person I date and has used his ghostly powers to ruin a few occasions."

"Ghostly powers, huh?" Bonnie laughed. "I guess that could be good or bad."

"It's been good a few times. He's saved my life more than once. But I've saved him too. I think we're even."

That same errant breeze that shouldn't have been inside the pickup gently moved Stella's pony tail.

"Is he disagreeing?"

"He's always disagreeing."

Bonnie told her about seeing Eric's picture at the firehouse. "He looks just like by brother. You don't think there's any chance..."

Stella turned her head. "Well, Romeo?"

There was no sound from the back seat where she looked. Bonnie hoped to be able to see the infamous Sweet Pepper ghost at some point.

"He doesn't seem quite sure," Stella admitted. "What does your mother say?"

"I haven't asked her yet. She did say he paid her a call the night before he left town. While he was gone, she got married, and Eric was born the next year—maybe appropriately named."

"Is your brother at your house?" Stella asked. "Eric would like to see him."

"Sorry. You just missed him, but he's supposed to fly home for Christmas. Maybe we can get them together then. Would he be able to tell if my brother is his son using his ghostly powers?"

"Who knows? He's kind of freaked out about the whole idea from the look on his face."

Bonnie glanced in the rear view mirror. "Does he look like he did in the picture? Or is he like something you'd see at Halloween?"

"Nope." Stella laughed. "He's a big, strong, handsome devil who never has to worry about changing his clothes or combing his hair. I guess that's one advantage to being dead."

They talked about Christmas trees the rest of the way to the house. Stella wanted two blue spruce trees each about six feet tall. One was for the firehouse, and the other was for her cabin.

Rose came out when the two vehicles pulled up in the yard. She waved excitedly and came down the steps with slippers on her feet. "Oh my goodness. It's been so long since I saw you last. I'm so glad you're here."

Stella and Bonnie exchanged looks.

"Are you talking to Chief Griffin, Mom? Have you two met?" Bonnie asked.

"I know Chief Griffin," Rose said. "I was talking to Eric, of course. You know, I thought we were going to be married one day. But that was a long time ago. Still, it's good to see you."

"Can she really see him?" Bonnie asked.

"She's looking right at him." Stella nodded to the space on her right. "Believe me. He sees her too."

It was odd watching her mother have a conversation without seeing or hearing anyone she was talking to. If Bonnie didn't know about the ghost, she would have assumed the worst. As it was, she stood there while her mother spoke to Eric Gamlyn and they all watched.

"Wow. That's amazing," Petey said.

"That's the way Chief Gamlyn is sometimes," Ricky added. "We can't see him or hear him, but we can see her arguing with him."

Stella was affronted by that remark. "I'm always very careful where I speak to him."

Petey and Ricky nudged each other with their elbows and laughed.

"Right, Chief," Ricky said.

"Come on, Mom," Bonnie said. "Let's get inside. It's cold out here, and you don't have a coat or shoes. I'm sure Eric can go inside and talk for a bit."

Stella shook her head. "He can't go without me."

"Maybe you could just give her his badge until you're ready to go," Bonnie suggested.

"I'm sorry." Stella wasn't willing to do that. "Ricky and Petey know what we're looking for. I'll go inside with your mother, and they can pick out the trees."

"Wonderful!" Rose exclaimed. "Maybe you'd like a hot cup of cider, Chief Griffin."

The two women went inside. Bonnie laughed when she saw the door stay open just for a moment longer than it should have after they were already in the house. Were there things going on like that all around her, but she'd never noticed?

Petey and Ricky both grabbed an ax to cut down the Christmas trees. As soon as the trees were chosen, they engaged in friendly but fierce competition to see who could fell their tree the fastest. Bonnie was surprised when Petey won.

"Let's take them over to the bailer," Bonnie suggested. "Then we can get them loaded up."

There was a snowball fight and a race to see who could get their tree to the Jeep the fastest. It was clear there was a rivalry between Stella's two co-assistant chiefs—and something more.

"That's it," Bonnie said. "You're ready to go."

They went inside, where Stella and Rose both had cups of cider in front of them at the kitchen table. There was a full cup of cider at the seat next to Rose's. Bonnie assumed that's where Eric was sitting.

"Not there!" Rose said as Ricky started to sit in that spot.

"Sorry, ma'am." He glanced at the empty chair. "Sorry, Chief Gamlyn."

Rose got Ricky and Petey cups of hot cider and brought out a pan of s'mores. She carefully put one of the confections on a napkin in front of Eric's seat.

They talked about the snow and touched on Harvey's death in the next thirty minutes they were there. Stella finally looked at her watch and said it was time for them to go.

"Please come back and visit anytime," Rose invited. "And be sure to bring Eric. He likes you very much, you know."

Stella smiled and nodded. "Sometimes, Miss Rose, when he's not annoyed and stomping around the cabin. Thanks for your hospitality. How much do I owe you for the trees, Bonnie?"

She started to say no charge then remembered what Matthew had said about the tree farm staying in business. She didn't want her brother to come home over Christmas and rant about them not making enough money. She quoted the standard price with a ten percent discount, since it was for the fire brigade.

"Thanks." Stella gave her the cash. "See you soon. Maybe we can have lunch one day in Sweet Pepper."

Rose applauded. "Oh yes! That would be fun. Can we eat at the cafe? That's Eric's favorite."

"Of course. Why not?" Stella smiled at Bonnie. "Let's do it once this snow is gone."

"Sure." Bonnie agreed. "See you later. Nice to meet you, Petey."

After they were gone, Bonnie cleaned up in the tree area so it was ready for the group that was coming. She walked through the fragrant lines of fir trees, inhaling deeply of their scent as she brushed her hands along the soft needles. It was something she'd enjoyed doing as a child. The smell was calming to her. Nothing else in the world had that effect.

She walked a long way, conscious of the time before she started back. Her nose and fingers were cold, but she felt wonderfully invigorated, more than she had in years. It was good to be home.

The stag she'd seen earlier walked into her path. She knew this was the same one she'd seen two days ago when a short Cherokee man followed him, carrying a wood staff. He wore a white robe that went to the ground. He appeared ancient, with a heavily wrinkled and wizened face. His hair was almost as long as the robe he wore and just as white.

"Good afternoon, Unega Awinita." He bowed his head to her. "We have much to speak of this day."

## Chapter Thirteen

Bonnie had left her gun in the house. She wasn't on duty, but she knew she should always be prepared. Trouble didn't respect her time off. Still, she didn't get that kind of impression from him. He looked harmless.

"I mean you no harm, Unega Awinita."

"I'm sorry. I think you have me confused with someone else. I'm Bonnie Tuttle. This is my family's Christmas tree farm. Would you like a tree?"

"Why should I cut a tree when I have them all for my enjoyment?" He raised his staff high as he spoke and cast an eye upon the forest around him.

She shivered, as the trees did, at his words. An eerie feeling seeped into her.

The old man put his hand on the stag's neck. "Something puzzles you?"

"Only why you're here. What can I do for you, sir?"

He laughed as he stroked the stag's neck. "She asks

what she can do for us, when it is we who have come to help her."

The big stag snorted and nodded its massive head, as though he was laughing with the old man. He pawed the ground, plumes of his breath freezing in the air.

"Okay. I'll bite. What have you come to help me do? And why are you calling me Unega Awinita?" Bonnie stared them both down as she tried to understand what was going on.

"We have come to help you protect all creatures in the wild, as you were meant to do." He continued to smile at her. "As for your name, it is as it has always been. We call you the white fawn when you return to us, as you have since before time began."

Weirder still. She put her hands in her pockets and tried to think what to say next. Obviously this was some mistake, or he was expecting someone else. Maybe he even got the idea because she was a Wildlife Agent. Anything was possible.

He hadn't tried to hurt her or the stag. She needed to reason with him, sure she could convince him that he was confused. She could ask him in for some hot cider. They could talk, and he could tell her where he lived.

"I see you are confused." He graciously bowed his head again to her. "We have a tale in these mountains. It is of a young, white woman who has endured great sorrow and has used her pain to help those around her. She has been reborn to us many times as Unega Awinita—the white fawn. She speaks with the wolves and the deer. She hears even the tiniest cries of the turtle and the chipmunk. She has compassion for them all and is their great protector."

Bonnie closed her mouth when she realized it was

open after hearing the story. She wasn't sure what to say next and decided against inviting him into her home. He might be dangerous. What if he decided she wasn't doing her job as a great protector?

"I see. What's your name? Where do you live? Can I call someone for you?"

Again he laughed at her. With an agility that should've been beyond him, the Cherokee man leapt on the back of the stag. "What is my name? You may call me sun, moon, or rain. Where do I live? I live here in the woods, free of restraint or understanding. I need no one but you by my side. Together we will protect the weak."

The old man nodded to the stag, and the animal bounded away through the field of Christmas trees.

She hadn't been sure when she'd first seen him on the road coming into Sweet Pepper, but this time she knew he was real. He was probably crazy or demented. She hoped she could ask around and find out if anyone else knew him.

"There you are." Matthew came running through the trees leading to her from the house. "Your group of Christmas tree hunters are here. I should have taken them for myself, but I did the honorable thing of coming to get you because Rose asked. Next time, they'll be buying my trees."

Bonnie was stumped for what to say. She stood there staring at him, wanting to tell him what she'd just seen but not finding the words that wouldn't make her sound crazy.

"Are you okay?" He came closer. "You look strange. You're not going to faint or anything are you? Are you sick?"

"No." She finally got one word out and shook her

head to clear it. "I just saw an old man and a big stag."

"Why didn't you say so? I didn't know you were looking for symbolism out here. The last vision I had in my trees was a bluebird. Obviously it wasn't real since it was winter, but I'm still trying to figure out what it means."

She grabbed his jacket lapels. "No. Really. There was a little old Cherokee man in a white robe riding a huge stag."

"Maybe you should go inside and have some hot cider. I'll take care of your tree buyers. You've been through a lot since you got here."

Bonnie let go of his jacket. "Sorry. Maybe that's it. I don't know what to think. I saw him on my way into town. He called me Unega Awinita again today. I don't know what's wrong with me."

"He called you that?" He glanced around. "Where is he? Where did he go?"

"Not you too. I'm not encouraging delusion. Let's go back to the house before my sale drives away."

Matthew put his hands on her arms. "Is it that you know the legend? Because I don't think he'd call you Unega Awinita. Although the animals listen to you." He stared hard into her face. "Are you the white fawn?"

"Are you making fun of me?" she demanded hotly. "I didn't ask for this to happen—and I'm not completely sure it did. But you aren't allowed to make fun of me about it."

"Yoo-hoo!" a woman sang out from the end of the row of trees. "Are you Bonnie Tuttle? We'd like to get our trees and get out of the valley before dark, please."

"I'm not making fun of you, Bonnie," Matthew said. "Really. We should talk about this."

"After I sell my trees." She glared at him. "But there better not be a smile on your face when we talk about it."

"There won't be." He followed her down the row toward the other woman. "Okay, maybe there will be, but I won't be making fun of you. I swear."

"We'll see," she promised and then smiled as she greeted her customer. "I'm so glad you could make it. Let's get those trees ready."

Matthew helped with the trees, though she didn't really need it. Mrs. Barnes had brought three big students to help load the truck. Bonnie thought it might be possible that Matthew didn't want to leave until he talked to her. He kept glancing at her as he was working.

She should never have told him. It had just made it worse.

When all fourteen trees were loaded and paid for, Bonnie dropped down on the front steps, exhausted. It was a good day for sales, but she was using muscles she hadn't used in a while cutting and loading trees. Of course, she'd also been knocked around by Vince Stookey too. No wonder she was sore and tired.

"I want you to tell me everything that Dustu said to you." Matthew sat next to her. "No one has seen him in years. Some thought he was dead. I thought he was only a legend."

"I don't want to talk about that right now," she replied. "Maybe tomorrow."

"This is a big deal, Bonnie. Everyone is going to want to know about it."

His words made her cringe. "Please don't tell anyone else. I don't care if other people want to know. I just want to forget about it and sit by the fire looking at Harvey's files."

"Tonight, right? Tomorrow we can tell everyone."

"No. I don't ever want to tell anyone but you, and I wouldn't have told you if it wasn't so astonishing at the time. I'm a private person, Matthew. I don't want to be laughed at or made fun of by everyone."

His dark eyes challenged hers. "That's asking a lot. But I'll go along with it, since I'm sure you'll change your mind. It's a huge honor to be addressed as Unega Awinita by one of our elders. It's not a title given lightly."

"I understand." She got up slowly from the stairs as Peter ran out of the house. "I'll see you tomorrow. Bye, Peter."

The boy had been with Rose again while his father had been helping her. Bonnie waved as they got in the truck and left the house. Then she went inside, took off her jacket and tennis shoes, and sat down by the fire.

"What should we eat for dinner tonight?" her mother asked.

"Something hot," Bonnie replied sleepily. "With something hot to drink. I'm still freezing."

* * *

It was dark outside when she woke. The clock on the mantel struck seven p.m. Bonnie yawned and got to her feet.

The little wolf sat silently between her and the kitchen.

"What are you doing in here? How did you get out of the kennel?"

"Oh. You're finally awake," Rose said. "I've had your dinner warming on the stove. I was starving and ate without you, I'm afraid. But I'll sit with you while you eat. Is your wolf hungry?"

"He's not my wolf. Did you let him out of his kennel?" She walked to her coat hanging by the door and pulled out the lock.

"No, but he's been very good just watching you sleep. Do you think he'd eat a corn fritter? I don't know if beans would be good for him. I have a lovely Apple Brown Betty made too, but probably not for the wolf."

The wolf still didn't move. He stared at Bonnie with great intent. He wasn't old enough to hunt, not that he would hunt in this environment. She was surprised he wasn't hiding or looking for a way out of the house.

"Are you hungry?" she asked him.

He licked his lips but otherwise stayed still.

"I think that's a yes," Rose said. "I've got some leftover chicken. I bet he'd like that."

"All right. Thanks. Let me get him in the laundry room again."

"He probably won't go with you if you don't have the chicken," Rose instructed.

"We'll see." Bonnie started walking toward the hall. The little wolf followed on her heels like a puppy. She looked in the kennel. The door was open, but she couldn't understand how. "If you're hungry, you have to go back in there."

She stood to one side and the pup went back in the kennel and sat down, as though he'd only come to get her and let her know that he was hungry. She smiled and put on her gloves to feed him. He looked healthy enough. Maybe she should let him out on his own in the next few days. She didn't know why, but he seemed already attached to her. Before she left, she latched the kennel and locked it, slipping the key onto her keyring.

Bonnie sat down to eat after that. Rose sat with her,

and they talked about ordinary things. The corn fritters were delicious, and so was the apple brown Betty. The kitchen was attached to the dining room and living room. She could still hear the crackling fire in the hearth. It was exactly what she needed to take a deep breath and relax after the insanity that had been the last two days.

"Matthew Brown Elk and his brother are very nice," Rose commented with a cup of tea in her hand. "It was such a shame when little Peter's mother decided to leave. How could anyone leave their child?"

"People do crazy things sometimes," Bonnie said. "There isn't always a way to understand it."

Her mother sighed. "What about that man you were seeing in Alabama? Was he nice? Is he going to come after you?"

"He was very nice." Bonnie smiled when she thought about Saul Chase. "He's not going to come after me. He's in love with someone else. That happens too sometimes. We don't always love the right people, do we?"

"No." Rose's gaze was soft and far away. "The heart doesn't always want what it can have."

Bonnie leaned closer to her mother.

"Was Eric Gamlyn my brother's father?" she asked softly. There was no one else to hear it but it seemed like a subject that should be discussed quietly.

"Yes."

Unsure how to respond, Bonnie tried to mirror her mother's calm demeanor. She had expected to have to work on her a little to get the answer, but instead Rose just sat there, sipping her tea.

"Eric never knew. He left the next day and was gone for a long time. I didn't know how to get in touch with him—no cell phones in those days." Rose smiled. "Not that I'm complaining. I loved Wendel too but in a different way. Before you ask, he knew that he wasn't Eric's father. He didn't care. He was a father to my son. That was all that mattered."

"Wow. Have you told my brother about this?"

"No." Rose held her pink mouth primly. "Why stir up old, painful memories? That's why I never told Chief Gamlyn when he came back. My life had moved on. I wanted to tell him, but it seemed too late. It would have only been confusing for our Eric."

Bonnie took it all in but found it difficult to believe that her mother had held such a huge secret inside her for so long. She covered Rose's delicate hand with her own larger, callused one.

"Now what about you?" Rose asked. Her eyes had lost that dreamy expression. "Have you moved on with your life, sweetheart? Have you put all your painful memories behind you?"

"I put that behind me when I left the valley ten years ago."

"Does that mean you've made peace with it, or is it going to haunt you now that you're back?"

"I don't know." Bonnie sipped her tea. "Even in Alabama, not a day went by when I didn't think about how old my baby would have been if he'd survived. It's not something you can forget—losing a child—even though I didn't know him. He was still part of me."

Rose gripped her daughter's hand tightly. "You have to move on too. I know it was hard on you. I understand why you left. All those old ladies gossiping about you and the baby, and you barely out of high school."

A lump formed in Bonnie's throat and tears came to her eyes. It still hurt after all this time.

"What about him?" Rose asked. "Do you ever hear from him?"

"No."

*Him* was, of course, the baby's father. Bonnie didn't know if her mother had ever said her boyfriend's name out loud after finding out that she was pregnant. Davis Leon. They'd dated through high school after growing up together in the valley. On graduation night, they'd driven into Pigeon Forge and rented a hotel room. It had all been very romantic and seemed legitimate since they'd been planning their wedding for months.

But as soon as she'd found out she was pregnant, Davis had advised her to get rid of it. He'd said a baby would only ruin their chances for the future.

Brokenhearted that he could so easily choose to end the life of their child, Bonnie had told him she never wanted to see him again with all the passion and drama of her eighteen-year-old heart. He'd begged her to reconsider. But she'd told him she and their baby were a package deal.

Davis had left town the next day—with his parents' blessing. They'd said it was all her fault, that she'd seduced their son with the idea of trapping him in marriage. Word had spread quickly, and Bonnie had to endure long months of coping with Davis's betrayal and her old friends taunting and belittling her.

All that had come to an end the night her baby was born. It was too early for him, the doctor had said. He'd never had a chance to live.

"I'm so glad you're back," Rose said. "I can't tell you how much I hated that you left to train as a Wildlife

Agent so quickly after the baby's death. You had no time to mourn. There were so many times I wished I could have held you in my arms and comforted you."

Bonnie forced herself not to cry. She'd cried rivers and oceans over that part of her life in the last ten years. The hurt never went away.

"I love you, Mom. And I'm a different woman now. I don't care about small-town gossip anymore. I'm ready to get on with my life from here."

"That's wonderful." Her mother got up to clear the table. "Because Matthew Brown Elk and his brother are both single."

"Really?" Bonnie laughed, the tension broken. "Matchmaking already?"

## Chapter Fourteen

Bonnie spent the rest of the evening looking through Harvey's papers. There was nothing in any of them about finding a ruby. She really didn't think there would be. Tomorrow she'd ask his family if they knew about the ruby and his plans for the future. She looked up rubies that had been found in North Carolina and Tennessee. There had been several stones found in the Smoky Mountains that had been worth some money. Most of them weren't recent finds. She wondered exactly how big a ruby would be that would allow Harvey to purchase a million-dollar beach house?

It made sense that he was going to retire if he thought he had a fortune. Where had he kept the stone? Had he showed it around town to people like Vince who wanted to get part of the fortune?

Around midnight, she went to bed and fell asleep right away. She had a strange dream about Eric Gamlyn.

He was cooking something in her mother's kitchen. He was tall and strong with her brother's bright blond hair and unearthly blue eyes.

He turned when she walked into the kitchen. "Good morning. Pancakes for breakfast?"

She woke up just as she was about to answer.

It wasn't surprising that she'd dreamed about Stella's ghost. Just the subtle hints of movement where there shouldn't have been and Stella's jacket flying up in the back seat of the jeep on her cue was enough to convince her. Not that she was difficult to convince. She'd grown up in the mountains with Native American lore and magic alongside mountain magic.

The dim light coming from the windows in her bedroom told her it was morning even before she glanced at the clock on her dresser. The light also picked out a visitor she hadn't expected.

"I can't believe you got out of the kennel again," she said to the wolf, who was sitting on her bed. "I think you might be magical too. I know wolves are smart, but I don't know if they're that smart."

The little wolf took that as an invitation to lie down. He curled up on her blanket, his nose touching his tail, his eyes watching her.

"You definitely need to be reintegrated into the wolf population. Maybe you're confused. I might be able to help you find your parents. Because wolves don't live in houses with people and they don't sleep on their beds." Bonnie shook her head and smiled. "And I'm talking to you. Let's get up and make breakfast for Mom for a change."

But even though it was early, Rose was already in the kitchen smiling and humming as she cooked. It made a shiver run down Bonnie's spine when her mother turned and said, "Good morning. Pancakes for breakfast?"

It was exactly like her dream except it was her mother instead of Eric Gamlyn.

"Is something wrong?" Rose asked, a frown developing between her fine brows.

"No." Bonnie poured coffee into cups for both of them. "I woke up having a strange dream and found the wolf on my bed. I don't understand how he's getting out of the kennel."

"I'm sure you'll figure it out. Sit down and eat some pancakes first. I'm sure you have a busy day ahead of you."

Bonnie grabbed some chicken pieces out of the fridge and went to the laundry room. The door to the kennel was open. "Okay. You know the drill. Get back inside, and I'll feed you."

The wolf sniffed and seemed to nod before he went back inside.

She closed the kennel door without feeding him. He stared at her inquisitively, cocking his head to one side.

"Let's see if we can figure out how you're doing this." She put the chicken pieces on the floor outside the kennel. The idea was that he'd escape to get the chicken and she could figure out what he was doing. She sat cross-legged on the floor and waited.

He stared back at her, waiting too.

"Bonnie," her mother called. "Your pancakes are getting cold. What are you doing back there?"

"I'll be there in a minute, Mom. I'm trying to figure this out."

Fifteen minutes later, she was still waiting—and so

was the wolf.

Her cell phone rang from her bedroom. She ignored it. Then the house phone rang.

"It's that nice police chief from Sweet Pepper," her mother called. "I ate your pancakes, but I'm making more. Are you almost done?"

Bonnie sighed. So much for her experiment. She put on the gloves and gave the chicken to the wolf, making sure to latch and lock the kennel. Not that it would do any good. "There you go. I guess you're too smart for me. Enjoy your breakfast. And if you can understand me—stay in your kennel. It won't be long now, and you'll be free again."

He stared at her a moment longer before he started eating. She got off the floor as there was a knock on the front door. Rose answered it and happily allowed Matthew into the house. Bonnie, who was still in her pajamas, scooted quickly into her bedroom and closed the door to get dressed.

By the time she'd come out, Matthew was already on his second plate of pancakes. Rose was delighted to have people to feed and was happily making more.

"Good morning," he said cheerfully when he saw Bonnie. "I thought I'd let my brother handle a few sales today and tag along with you."

Great. She sat at the table across from him and thanked her mother when she put down another plate of pancakes for her.

"What about Peter?" she asked as she tried to think of a nice way to tell him that she didn't want to talk about the old Cherokee man or her magical relationship with animals.

"School went back today. I already dropped him off.

I thought you could use the company and maybe you might need a good tracker since you're still looking for the person who killed Harvey and you haven't been around for a while. The area has changed. You might get lost."

"Isn't that nice?" Rose smiled at Matthew. "You'd make someone a wonderful husband."

Bonnie kept her head down and ate her pancakes. Maybe if she ignored her mother's matchmaking, it would stop.

"Well, Bonnie," Rose said. "Are you going to thank Matthew for his very generous offer to show you around the area while you're working?"

Her phone rang again. Chief Rogers sounded put out that he had to call back. "Crime scene is done with your Hummer. You can get it whenever you're ready. Have you spoken with Harvey's family about the ruby and the beach house?"

"Not yet, but I'm on my way over there."

"Better find another driver. Max towed your pickup, but that still leaves you with two vehicles to get to your place—unless you want to leave the Hummer with me. Stella has practice today. I have some info from the coroner too."

Bonnie glanced up at Matthew, who was grinning. Chief Rogers had a loud voice. She was sure he could hear him speaking.

"I'll take care of it. Thanks, Chief." She ended the call and put the phone in her pocket. "Did you know about this?"

"How could I? I can't keep up with the crime scene people. Let's just call it an educated guess."

"I'd say that works out for the best," Rose said. "If

we get any tree customers, I'll give you a call. Have a good day."

"I'll be back for lunch," Bonnie told her as she got to her feet. "Thanks for breakfast. I'll bring something home for lunch."

"Don't be silly. You know I love to cook. Maybe you could help me. You were a very good cook when you lived at home. Men really like women who can cook."

Okay. Maybe she couldn't wait for her mother's matchmaking to go away. It was already embarrassing. Bonnie wasn't ready for a new relationship yet. She was still getting over Saul.

"All right. Well, I'll see you later anyway. Call if you need anything."

"Maybe some chicken," Rose said. "That little wolf has quite an appetite."

Bonnie and Matthew said goodbye and went out to her brother's truck.

"I have to see Harvey's family before I go to Sweet Pepper." She opened the driver's side door.

"I know. I heard what Chief Rogers said."

She started the engine. "I don't want to talk about your tribal elder and his ideas about me."

"Sure. I understand." He chuckled.

"What's so funny?"

"I think you may have picked up some hitchhikers without realizing it." He nodded to the hood.

There were three hawks standing on the hood staring at her. One of them was holding his wing at an unnatural angle.

"What are they doing?" she asked.

"You told me not to talk about it."

Bonnie frowned at him. "I don't understand."

"I'd say they're looking for Unega Awinita. One of them needs help. The old stories tell of the animals coming to the white fawn when they were injured. But you told me not to tell you that."

She left the engine running and got out of the truck. The three brown-tailed hawks swiveled their bodies as she moved so they were still facing her. The one with the injured wing stepped away from the other two, closer to her. His head moved so that he was looking at her closely.

"Even if I wanted to, I don't know how to set a wing," she told Matthew as he got out and stood beside her in the snow. "We're taught to help injured animals but not specific things like that. Besides, it would probably fly up and peck out my eyes if I tried to touch it."

The hawk, as though understanding her dilemma, jumped on her arm, its talons lightly holding on to her. Bonnie was startled but stayed very still. The bird stayed where it was.

"Okay." She watched it suspiciously. "Any suggestions?"

"How different could it be than setting a human arm?" Matthew was still grinning.

"My mother has some art supplies in the house," she told him. "See if she has a popsicle stick. Maybe that would work, though I don't know how I'll keep it in place."

Matthew did her bidding and returned with her mother, some twine, and a thinner piece of wood than a popsicle stick.

"Oh my stars!" Rose exclaimed when she saw the hawk on her daughter's arm. "Remember that time you tried to help the baby sparrow that fell out of the nest too early."

"He died, Mom," Bonnie said. "Maybe not a good example."

She moved very slowly and carefully to hold the hawk's wing in her free hand. "I'm sorry I'm hurting you. There might be a better choice of human to take care of this for you."

The hawk screeched but didn't move.

"I think he wants you," Matthew said. "He seems pretty sure about it. I wish I had my phone. I could take a picture of this and send it to Facebook. Thomas and I share one so he gets it when he's working."

"Probably not a good idea anyway," Bonnie said as she looked at the injured wing. She straightened out the wing, got the thin slice of wood next to it, and attached the wood with the twine. "I don't think you're going to do any flying with this," she warned the hawk. "But maybe it will help it heal right."

"Won't it die if it can't fly?" Rose asked.

"Maybe he'll come back and let me feed him," Matthew suggested. "Better make that more chicken than you planned for the wolf. Did you pick out a name for him yet?"

Bonnie held out her arm, and the two hawks that had remained with the injured one helped it glide up to the roof of the house near the chimney.

"No. He's not a pet." She rolled her eyes. "I'm going to look around the island today to see if I can find any wolf tracks. Maybe they'll lead me to his family, and I can reintegrate him."

"Good thing Thomas can get by without me today. I can see we're going to have a busy day."

## Chapter Fifteen

Bonnie stopped first at the old Wildlife Agent's office. Even though most of the snow had melted away, the place still looked rough. The roof not only sagged but had leaked badly as the sun had turned the snow into puddles of water.

"This is where they expect you to work?" Matthew asked as he glanced around the dilapidated building. "I think this used to be an old logging cabin. That means it's been here a long time."

"I'll say. We used to play here when we were kids. I suppose the state allowed the feds to use it so they wouldn't have to do anything with it."

"I'll help you fix it up, if you like. I have a friend with a bulldozer." He chuckled at his own joke.

"No thanks. It can fall down on its own. I just want to get Harvey's stuff out of here. I'm going to work in my brother's office at the house. At least there's running water there."

They gathered up everything they could find that seemed as though it could have something to do with Harvey's job as a Wildlife Agent. Bonnie was careful to look in every tiny place in the building where Harvey could have stored a large ruby.

"But why put it here?" Matthew asked. "Wouldn't he have kept it in a bank safety deposit box or something secure like that?"

"I don't know. I didn't know him well enough to say. It seems like he was hiding it, so maybe this would be a good spot." She put her hands on her hips as she looked around. "Maybe he thought no one would look here."

"And yet this must've been the first place Vince looked. Maybe it wasn't such a secret."

"Let's get the last of this stuff out of here, and we'll go ask his family. After that, we might know where the ruby is—if there really is a ruby."

"There must be." He hefted a large box of files and pictures, balancing it on his shoulder. "He had to figure he was buying that beach house with something."

Bonnie didn't disagree. When the office was clear of everything but useless debris, she closed the door, for all the good it did, and they got in the truck to head to Harvey's house.

"Looks like it's gonna be another good day for melting." Matthew glanced out the window at the ice and snow still dripping from the trees. "I hope that means tree sales are gonna pick up. Not long now until Christmas."

"I suppose there aren't many sales after that," she quipped.

"Then there's only work thinning the trees and planting new ones. None of the fun stuff until next year." He shook his head. "I noticed you have a large blue spruce in one of your fields. You might want to take a picture of it and see if the White House is interested. It's a big deal to be chosen. Your farm gets national attention, and you get a free trip to Washington to meet the big guy."

"My family had one, remember?" She smirked. "But I thought they came to you or something. I didn't know you had to submit something."

"Thomas wants to be on a plaque in the general store in the worst way."

"What about you?"

"It would be okay, I guess." He shrugged. "But it's a one-time shot. The real business is day in and day out. That's what I try to focus on."

They'd reached Harvey's house. Bonnie had planned to go inside alone to speak with Jean Shelton, but she and her children were getting ready to leave, which made her talk to them outside before they could go.

"I'm sorry to bother you again," Bonnie said. "I just have a question about your husband's plans to retire."

Mrs. Shelton was pale, her eyes red-rimmed from crying. "Yes? What possible difference do his retirement plans make now?"

"Chief Rogers learned that Harvey bought an expensive beach house on Hilton Head Island the same week he came to visit me in Alabama." Bonnie felt uneasy asking personal questions like this of a grieving widow. "The police want to know how he could afford something like that on a federal agent's salary."

"I just don't understand why that makes any difference now." Mrs. Shelton dabbed at her eyes with a tissue. "Harvey's dead. He's never going to see his dream come true."

"I really think you should look for my father's killer," Gerald said in a gruff voice. "Standing out here in the cold, asking my mother stupid questions when she's on her way to pick out my father's coffin, seems counterproductive, Agent Tuttle."

"She's just doing her job," Abigail argued. "This is how they find the person who killed Dad."

"Well, not right now." He opened the door of the SUV, whose engine was warming up in the driveway. "Come back later, Agent Tuttle. Have some answers for us, and maybe we'll have some answers for you."

As they were getting in the car, Bonnie poked her head in the open doorway by Harvey's widow in the back seat. "Did your husband mention that he found a large, valuable ruby? Did you know about that? It might be why he was killed."

Gerald instructed his mother to close her door. The SUV's tires spun up snow and gravel in his haste to get away.

"I'd say the son knows about the ruby and the beach house," Matthew said as she got back in the truck. "But not the mother or the daughter."

"How can you tell?" Bonnie asked, fastening her seatbelt.

"Well for one thing, it was good you weren't standing behind that SUV. I think he would've gone through you to get out of the drive. He doesn't exactly look innocent to me."

"Even if he knows about the ruby and the beach

house, that doesn't mean he killed his father."

"No. But he might have hired someone to do it."

"At this point, anything seems possible." She put the pickup in reverse and left the Shelton home.

Traffic was brisk going up and down the treacherous winding mountain road. Every sharp turn had a car or a truck in the other lane. Some people were better than others at staying on their side of the yellow line.

"I hope you've reconsidered letting me tell everyone that you've seen Dustu. People would be very excited to know someone had seen him."

"I don't want to spread around these ideas," she told him. "It's bad enough that you believe them."

"What's not to believe? Were there three hawks waiting for you on the truck this morning or not? Does the little wolf listen to you like you're his mother or not? These things don't just happen. If Dustu says you're the white fawn, you're the white fawn."

"That's what I'm talking about." She found a spot near town hall to park the truck for her meeting with Chief Rogers. "I don't want people waiting around to see what I'm going to do next. I just want to do my job."

"I understand, but—"

Bonnie opened the truck door to get out. "That's it. I really don't want to talk about it, and I don't want to see an article about it in the *Sweet Pepper Gazette*. I'm sorry, Matthew. I don't want people looking at my life that closely."

"I think you're wrong. Unega Awinita is a figure of hope. The return of our shaman is the same." He got out and closed the door. "I'm going to get some coffee while you talk to Chief Rogers."

She knew he was disappointed about not being able to spread the word, but her past had made her vulnerable to people speculating about her life. She never wanted people to spend time gossiping about her again.

Her mind in turmoil, Bonnie didn't see the woman standing at the door to town hall until she had almost walked into her. "Excuse me. I didn't see you."

The other woman was about her age with shoulder-length, brown hair and a white jacket with matching boots. "Oh, that's okay. I have whole days that go by, and I don't see anyone else."

"I know what you mean." Bonnie laughed and held the door open.

The woman suddenly turned back to her. "Is that you, Bonnie Tuttle? I thought it was you. I haven't seen you in years. Not since you left town after your baby died. Are you married now? Do you have other children?"

Keeping her head down, Bonnie just wanted to get past her. She thought the best way was to ignore her, but the other woman followed her past Sandie Selvie's desk.

"It's me, Lindsey Blake. You remember me. We used to hang out afterschool. I was the first person who knew you were dating Davis Leon. Remember?"

Bonnie stopped walking. She could see Lindsey's youthful face in the features of the woman before her. She was thinner now and looked tired. "Sure. I remember you. How have you been?"

"As good as someone can be who made the mistake of having two sets of twins right after each other." Lindsey rolled her expressive, brown eyes. "We should have lunch and catch up. Are you back in town to stay?"

Sandie and a few police officers were listening to their conversation. Bonnie reminded herself that this was bound to happen. She'd told her mother she was over it, the shame and anger of the past. But she'd lied. She was only over it if no one brought it up.

"That would be great." Bonnie was happy to see Chief Rogers come out of his office. "I'll call you. It was good to see you."

"But there's something else I should tell you," Lindsey continued. "And you don't have my number. Let me get my cell phone out."

"Mrs. Leon." Chief Rogers nodded to her. "I guess you and our new Wildlife Agent know each other, huh? I'm glad she has some friends here still. I hope she'll stick around for a while."

Bonnie hoped the shock from learning that Lindsey had married Davis didn't show on her face. She smiled woodenly. "So you married Davis. Congratulations. I remember him saying that twins ran in his family."

"Right this way, Bonnie," Chief Rogers said. "The coroner is here waiting."

"Wait a minute." Lindsey called out. "Let me get your phone number."

"Maybe later." Bonnie managed to say in a pleasant tone. "I'm sorry. I have to go."

"I would've told you if I knew how to get in touch with you," Lindsey's voice trailed off as Bonnie went into the conference room. "But we can still be friends."

Chief Rogers closed the door behind them. Bonnie wished she had more than a moment to gain some composure after meeting up with Lindsey again. But Judd Streeter was finishing a full breakfast at the conference table and sliding reports to her and the chief across the table.

"You two should order some breakfast from the cafe," the coroner said. "You both look like you could use some protein."

Bonnie took a deep breath, sat at the table, and began trying to make sense of the coroner's report. She'd have time to deal with her emotions later.

## Chapter Sixteen

But her mind kept whispering—Lindsey was going to spread this all over town. She was married to Davis, who thought he couldn't possibly want a child ten years ago and now had two sets of twins. So it wasn't kids he didn't want. It was her.

"Any questions, Agent Tuttle?" the coroner asked. "Hello?" he snapped his fingers. "I told you that you needed some protein."

"Sorry." Bonnie cleared her mind and stared at the report. "So nothing we didn't already suspect."

"That about sums it up." Chief Rogers closed the file on his copy of the report. "I don't see any ideas about Harvey being moved around God knows where."

"There were two buttons missing on his shirt, which could be accounted for by moving him. I didn't see him at the crime scene as I should have. I'm doing the best I can."

"If he'd burned up on the island, there wouldn't be anything to see," the chief reminded Judd and then glanced at Bonnie.

"I noticed that his buttons had been redone when he fell out of the Hummer," Bonnie told him. "I think I would have noticed his clothes being messed up that way at the island if it had happened there. He looked fine before he was shot."

Judd took a deep breath and exhaled loudly, clearly still irritated about the crime scene. He was dedicated to his job and didn't like things to be questionable. Too much could go wrong with his work.

"I haven't completed the work on Ray Hoy as yet, but he was definitely shot with a high-powered rifle from a distance of at least a hundred yards. Completely different from the up close and personal shooting with a .38 revolver that killed Harvey."

"It could still have been the same person," Bonnie suggested. "Maybe whoever it was shot Harvey and then got in a boat and joined the boats off the island. There were so many out there. I don't know if anyone would've noticed one extra while they were fighting the fire."

"Anything in the Hummer that shouldn't have been there?" the chief asked.

"No, sir. Agent Tuttle was lucky he wasn't killed in the vehicle—would've been a big mess to clean up out of that fine vehicle."

"Anything from Hoy's friend, Vince?" Bonnie asked.

"Not much," Chief Rogers replied. "He claims he was just checking things out at the office because he'd heard Harvey was dead and there might have been something he could pawn. I don't know yet. We've still got him."

John Trump came in quickly with a report of his own. "Sorry I'm late. I've been running all over town looking for the tires that match the prints we made. So far, too many match it. I don't know how to narrow it down. We've got a lot of vehicles in the area with seventeen-inch tires with that tread pattern. So far, all of them have come from the same tire store down at the county line."

"As for the bullet that was removed from the wolf after it passed through Harvey," Judd peered at them over his glasses, "it doesn't happen a lot that something surprises me but this did. Definitely Harvey's blood and tissue on the bullet. I assume that the wolf was kept for further study?"

"Further study?" Bonnie asked. "Why would you want to study him any further? You just said the bullet is the one that killed Harvey. What more would be gained by studying him?"

"If we opened him up, I might be able to get other blood and tissue samples from Harvey that were left in the wolf." Judd smiled. "Don't worry. We'll have him put down first. He won't feel a thing."

That made Bonnie angry. He wasn't taking her wolf to dissect.

*Her* wolf? What?

"These wolves are endangered in this area," she told him. "The pup is lucky to be alive as it is, after being burned and shot. I don't see any reason to sanction an autopsy on him to prove what you already know. The Wildlife Agency would fight you on that."

"You are an animal lover, aren't you?" Judd

laughed. "Harvey wasn't so strong about that. All right. Let's not make a big deal of it. I assume you're letting the wolf back in the wild once he heals."

"That's right," Bonnie said still bristling.

"What about the family?" Chief Rogers asked her. "Did you get a sense of whether or not they knew about the ruby and the beach house?"

She told him about her encounter with them. "The son was angry, but he's mourning too, so it's hard to say. None of them really answered my question."

"Let's get on that again," he said. "I'll give them a call later and have them come in."

"If that's it, I've still got an autopsy to finish." Judd's chair scraped across the wood floor as he got to his feet. "Good day."

"John, I know you were out there at the fire," the chief said. "But talk to Stella and everyone else from the fire brigade who were there. See if they noticed a boat that didn't belong. That could be our killer, at least one of them anyway."

"Yes, sir." John nodded to Bonnie and left the room.

"I know you've got a lot on your plate right now with just getting settled in," Chief Rogers said to Bonnie. "I appreciate all your help on this."

"Thanks. I don't feel like I can leave Harvey hanging without figuring out what happened to him."

He handed her the keys to the Hummer. "It's parked in the impound lot over on Fifth Street. Just tell Sparky I sent you. Let me know if you come up with anything else."

"I will." She put the keys in her pocket.

Bonnie left town hall after saying goodbye to Sandie. She didn't see Matthew outside as the strong wind whipped loose crystals of snow along the street. People hurried to get indoors, with their faces down and heavy clothes bundled around them.

A Santa rang a bell outside the cafe. Bonnie tossed some change into his bucket. The sign said the money was going to be used to help send the Sweet Pepper High School marching band to finals. The Santa thanked her and kept ringing his bell.

Inside the warm cafe, dozens of people huddled over their coffee and breakfast. The smell of biscuits was almost too good to resist. Voices were raised in conversation, and a radio was playing in the kitchen between cries of, "Order up!"

Bonnie looked around for Matthew. Despite herself, she was nervous standing there, hoping that no one else would ask about her past. She was about to turn and leave when Lucille Hutchins scooted toward her.

"Good morning. Say!" Lucille's blue eyes widened under her red hair. "You're the new Wildlife Agent, aren't you? Ricky Jr. told me all about you. He said you were pretty." She smiled. "I'll bet you're looking for Matthew and Stella, aren't you? They're right over there at that table." She pointed. "What can I get you to drink?"

"Coffee would be nice. Thanks." Bonnie was still cringing inside, feeling eyes on her from around the cafe after Lucille's loud welcome.

There was another man at the table with Matthew and Stella—Bonnie remembered him from yesterday—Walt Fenway. No doubt he and Matthew would want to talk about her special abilities with animals. She almost didn't join them.

But then Lucille saw her standing there again and

guided her to the spot, putting a cup of coffee in a plain mug before her. "There you go. What about some breakfast?"

"No thanks. I already ate."

Eggs, bacon, and toast were piled on Matthew's plate. How could he eat again so soon?

"Oh, honey," Lucille said. "You aren't gonna want to sit here with nothing while all your friends are eating. I'll bring you a biscuit—on the house, since you're new to Sweet Pepper."

What else could she say but thanks?

"Don't fight it." Stella picked up a biscuit from her plate. "Just plan on working out longer. That's what I do now. It got so bad I could hardly wear my jeans."

Bonnie smiled and sipped her coffee. Did they all know about the baby, Davis Leon, and why she left home ten years ago? Gossip travelled faster than the smell of fried chicken in Sweet Pepper and Christmas Tree Valley. It made her want to withdraw and get away again. It had been wonderful in Alabama, where no one knew anything about her.

"Hello," Walt said with a steady grin on his lined face. "We meet again. Small town, huh? Talk to any foxes today?"

"Not today," Matthew muttered. "It was hawks."

"What are the two of you talking about?" Stella glanced at Bonnie. "Do you know?"

Matthew opened his mouth to speak but was silenced by Bonnie's forbidding stare. "I better not say anything else. She carries a gun, you know."

"I've been shot before. I'm not afraid of it." Walt related his story about the fox to Stella and Matthew. "Isn't there a Cherokee name for someone who can talk to animals?"

"There is." Matthew nodded. "But I'm rather fond of my skin. I'm not saying anything else unless she says it's okay."

"So you speak with animals?" Stella smiled. "I speak with ghosts. I wonder if there's a name for that."

Bonnie took a deep breath. At least they weren't talking about her past. These stories about animals wanting her help and doing what she asked them to do were nothing.

"Speaking of which, I'm surprised you're sitting here with us since Eric is here," Stella changed the subject. "I thought you didn't like being around him."

"He's not here at the table," Matthew said. "I don't care if he's nearby."

"Can you see him?" Walt asked. "I'd give anything to see him and hear him again."

"It's more that I can feel him," Matthew replied. "It's uncomfortable but not so bad when he isn't up close in my face. I wish I could talk you out of having him around, Stella. Nothing good can come from being with a ghost."

Stella ignored him and washed down another bite of her biscuit with a sip of Coke.

"Anything you can gossip about from the meeting with the coroner and Chief Rogers this morning?" Walt asked Bonnie.

"There really wasn't much that he told us that we didn't already know." Lucille put down a small plate with a biscuit on it for her. "Thanks."

"So we still don't know why Harvey was killed or who did it." Walt sipped his coffee and shook his head. "In my day, we'd have some answers by now. I trained

Don Rogers to do a better job than this. What's that man thinking?"

Bonnie didn't volunteer any other information about the case. Like her past, everyone would be talking about it by the afternoon if she did. It would be better if everyone didn't know about Harvey's nest egg.

"I have to get back for training," Stella said. "I'm glad I'm not pulling sixty pounds of hose up a ladder today. Not with that biscuit in me."

"I'm coming too," Walt said, pushing out of the booth on the other side. "I love seeing those new recruits huffing and puffing."

"We should be going too." Bonnie took a last sip of coffee and wrapped the biscuit in a napkin before she put it in her jacket pocket. "You never know when you're going to run into a hungry animal who needs this more than me."

"We, huh?" Walt lifted his brows at the word. "You and Brown Elk travelling together?"

"I'm helping her bring the Hummer down to the valley today," Matthew defended. "She can only drive one vehicle at a time. Don't start with me, Walt. I don't want to hear that Bonnie and I are dating when I get home."

The older man laughed. "Your secret is safe with me, son. Don't worry about a thing."

"That's what bothers me," Matthew muttered.

The cashier rang up Stella's meal but refused to take any money from Bonnie because she was new to town. Bonnie and Stella ended up waiting at the door by themselves for Walt and Matthew to settle their bills.

"There's something I wanted to tell you," Bonnie said quietly. "But not in front of Walt and Matthew."

"What is it?" Stella asked with a concerned look on her pretty freckled face.

Bonnie told her the story of her brother Eric's conception. "I don't know if he's here with us, but I thought Chief Gamlyn might want to know that he has a son."

"Really?" Stella glanced to her left. "If he could do cartwheels right now, he would. Not having a family has hurt him a lot. This is great news for him. He wants to know where your brother is right now."

"Unfortunately, he's just taken a job overseas. But he'll be home for Christmas. Maybe we could get together then. It didn't surprise me after seeing Chief Gamlyn's picture at the firehouse. My brother looks just like him."

"He's very excited." Stella laughed. "Let's plan to do that when he gets back. He wants to know who your father is?"

"Barry Tuttle. My mother remarried after Wendel Harcourt died. My brother and I are almost twenty years apart."

"I'm sure you can imagine how sorry Eric is that he didn't know about his son while he was alive," Stella told her. "He's happy he knows the truth now but wonders why your mother didn't tell him."

"That's something I don't know for sure. She seemed to be able to see him. Maybe he could ask her next time they see each other." Bonnie grinned and shook her head. "Is this weird or what?"

"About as weird as people who can talk to animals. Don't worry. Your secret is safe with me. I can't say as much about Matthew or Walt."

"Too late to put that in the box, I guess."

Stella covered Bonnie's hand with hers and stared into her eyes. "Gossip is stupid, but it's what people do. It can only hurt you if you let it. I like you. Don't let it."

The way she said it, Bonnie knew that Stella was aware of her past. She swallowed hard and resisted the urge to run out to the truck and drive away. If Stella knew, so did Walt and Matthew. She couldn't put that back in the box either.

"Thanks. I'll do the best I can."

A warm feeling like standing in front of a heater blew around her. She could almost hear a whisper in one ear telling her that she would be okay.

"Eric is a big hugger now." Stella smiled. "You'd think his hugs would be cold, but they're warm, aren't they?"

## Chapter Seventeen

Tears stung Bonnie's eyes and clogged her throat for a moment at the idea that the ghost of the old fire chief had hugged her. Walt was complaining about the price of coffee, and Matthew was putting on his jacket. It gave her time to gain some composure.

"Hey." Matthew looked closely at her as they were leaving the cafe. "Are you okay? Did something happen between you and Stella?"

"Nothing bad. I'm fine. Let's get out to the lake and see if we can find the pup's family."

"I can't believe you haven't named him," he said as he swung his large body into the passenger seat of the truck. "He's not going to leave you. He belongs to you now, and you belong to him. Even if you find his family, they won't matter anymore. He won't stay with them."

"I've relocated gators, possums, and every other animal you can imagine," she told him, starting the truck. "I can relocate this wolf too."

He chuckled. "Not gonna happen."

They drove to the lake, talking about Christmas tree issues that she was unfamiliar with but knew she needed to understand since her brother was gone. There were new types of fertilizer and improved ways to help trees grow faster and stronger. She might have known some of them when she was much younger and liked to hear her father talk about the subject at dinner each night.

But she had only been eighteen when she'd left the valley. Training with the Wildlife Agency had crammed her head full of animal habitats, following trails, and what was good for maintaining adequate feeding grounds. She knew how to get a possum out of a trash can for its best interest, as well as excitable humans'. She could catch a bat as it flew out of a chimney and keep rabbits from eating garden lettuce.

She hoped those things would help her find the pup's family. They were going to have to go out to the island again to check where they could for wolf prints and habitat. She hoped the pup's family wasn't killed in the fire.

They'd reached the lake and left the truck behind on the shore.

"Any ideas where to look?" Matthew asked as he cast off from the dock.

"I remember people telling me what a great tracker you are," she reminded him, starting the engine on the boat that belonged to the Wildlife Agency.

"Oh." He raised his brows and grinned. "Are you offering me employment? I don't track for free, Agent Tuttle. A man who raises Christmas trees has to make money where he can."

"We'll see. I'd have to start an account for you with the agency."

"Done. I worked for Harvey many times. Look me up. I even have paper and electronic billing logos." He was obviously very proud of himself.

She gave in. "Okay. Let's see if we work well together."

"Have you ever worked with a tracker before?"

"I have. It didn't always work out, but sometimes it was useful."

"Good. Let's give it a whirl." His deep brown eyes caught hers. "Because I think you and I could be very good together, Unega Awinita."

Her heart skipped a beat, and then she broke eye contact with him. She focused on the ravaged island that was coming up quickly. "It looks worse than I thought."

There were a few tall pines still standing, still reaching toward the bright blue, winter sky. They bore scars of what they'd endured, but they'd probably continue to grow. The rest of the undergrowth and shorter trees were charred and blackened. No smoke still rose from the burned earth. That was good news. Stella and her crew had done a fine job of clearing out the hot spots.

"Look!" Matthew pointed to an eagle that perched on one of the surviving trees. "A good sign."

"It's easy for them. They can just fly away. It's the smaller animals that get trapped."

But there were already signs that other animals had returned as well. Bonnie pointed to dozens of mouse tracks on the shore. A few possums stared at them from a sawed-off log at the edge of the woods.

"This is where we docked when we got here."

Bonnie pointed to the old pier that showed no signs of having been touched by the fire. "A few yards from here is where I found the pup and Harvey."

"So the boat was moored here when Ray Hoy was shot out of it, right?" he asked, glancing out at the lake.

"But there were dozens of boats out here. The *Tennessee Teardrop* coordinated everything, but it was like any other response from a volunteer rescue group. Even people off duty show up. I don't know if anyone can tell us exactly who was out here."

"And who shot Ray," he concluded. "I get it." He jumped into the water and pulled the boat in so it could be tied to the old dock.

Bonnie jumped in too after cutting the engine as the boat came near shore. She could still see a few footsteps on the shore that might belong to her, Harvey, or Ray Hoy. Or any number of people who were here that day.

They waded ashore and began looking for any clues that could lead them to information about other wolves living on the island.

"He's too young to have been living on his own," Matthew said. "His parents probably were here, but they probably swam away and accidentally left him behind, especially if there was more than one pup."

Even though so much snow had fallen, the island was nearly free of it, either from the heat of the fire during the snowfall or the high winds after it. Bonnie easily found the spot where she'd encountered Harvey's body and a few yards away, the wounded pup.

"I wonder if the coroner has been out here," he said. "There might still be some valuable evidence."

"I'll suggest that," she replied. "I don't think he's been out here. He was pretty disgusted that the body had been moved so much."

"Yeah. That sounds like him."

They continued walking away from the two spots of blood on the rocky-sandy ground. Matthew pointed out places where animals had escaped across the shore during the fire. Bonnie saw them too—paw prints from a beaver, a raccoon, and more mice.

"Was there more blood where you found Harvey?" he asked. "It didn't look like much."

"No, I don't think he was shot out here. I don't know why the pup followed since he was shot at the same time. But I think Harvey was closer to the woods."

"Like this?" He pointed to a larger amount of dried blood on stones and leaves right next to the tree line.

"I think so." She stopped to take several pictures. "There was no time to look around that day."

"I guess not. You didn't know if you were going to burn with it."

"What's that?" Bonnie got closer to the bloody site Matthew was carefully examining without touching. She put on latex gloves and handed him her phone to document what she was doing.

"Looks like a red jeweler's bag." He snapped a picture every few seconds. "Maybe the ruby is in there and he just dropped it trying to get away from the fire. If I had something like that, I'd keep it on me all the time."

She examined the velvet bag that was crusted with Harvey's blood. "It's flat. There's nothing in it now."

"Shake it out to be sure. We don't know how big a million-dollar ruby is, do we?"

Bonnie did as he suggested, but nothing came out of the bag. "Maybe whoever killed him already took the ruby."

"Then he's long gone—unless it was Ray Hoy."

"No. He was by the boat when we pulled up. Harvey was still with me."

Matthew crouched close to the area they were studying. "Unless the ruby just fell out and it's red so we can't see it in all this."

"Give Chief Rogers a call, would you? I think we need the coroner out here right now."

They didn't go near the site again, just stayed on the island to make sure no one else bothered it either.

Matthew picked out the wolf pup's paw prints as he emerged from the tree line. His footsteps were tinged with his blood. They followed them backwards and managed to find the den. It appeared that there could have been more than one pup. But even though they fanned out from the den, the fire had been too hot here to track the animals.

"We won't find them this way unless we see their prints headed to the water on the shore," Bonnie said. "The ash is too deep."

"I don't see anything to suggest that they didn't escape," he said. "They'll probably come back at some point, but it may be a while. I guess they swam to the mainland to get away from the fire. Your pup was caught in what happened to Harvey, and the mother left him to save the other pup."

"I'm pretty sure there's a healthy wolf population around here. They'll take him in once he's healed." She stared past the water to Sweet Pepper, where the trees still had some snow on them. It was a stark difference between that shore and the island.

They heard the sound of the engine powering the

boat as it headed toward them. Matthew pointed to the mid-sized craft that was coming across the still lake. Chief Rogers was bringing the coroner to the island in the police boat.

"I'll bet that's one unhappy man," Bonnie suggested. "I don't think he planned to come out here at all."

"He's okay once you get to know him." Matthew grinned. "If you don't expect too much."

Chief Rogers threw Matthew the mooring line to the boat so he could pull the craft to shore. There was no point in the newcomers wading away from the boat since the two of them already had wet pants legs.

"I don't see how we're supposed to find much here after there was a fire," Judd Streeter complained after he was off the boat.

"Don't get all worked up," Chief Rogers said. "No one is asking you to go into the interior of the island. Agent Tuttle said the crime scene is at the edge of the forest."

The coroner hefted his leather bag and shrugged. "So where's my crime scene?"

Bonnie took him to the spot they'd found. She gave him the red velvet jewelry bag. "We think this is where Harvey was killed. You can see the spot over there where the pup was shot too. His den was just beyond that spot, and this is where he would've tried to run to the water."

"An assumption that might be aided if I'd examined the animal," Streeter complained. "Without that, it's all hearsay."

But he sat down in the sand and was eventually on his knees gathering evidence from the rocks, sand, and flora around the bloody area.

"Are you thinking someone dragged Harvey from that spot?" Chief Rogers asked Bonnie.

"No, sir. I think he probably crawled, though it's hard to tell since the shore is such a mess from animals running through to the lake."

He nodded. "Let's hope Judd can get a good print from that velvet bag. It might be all we have to go on."

"We would've heard rumors if someone had stolen the ruby from Harvey and tried to sell it," Matthew pointed out. "Something of that worth wouldn't be ignored."

"Unless the weather has kept the killer from getting out to make the sale," Chief Rogers suggested. "Let's face it. The killer isn't gonna get top dollar for a gemstone here in Sweet Pepper."

"Good point," Bonnie agreed. "So where would they go?"

"In Tennessee, I'd think Nashville or across into North Carolina. I'm not really sure," the chief admitted. "I've put out some feelers to gemstone dealers that I know. Like everything else right now, we're just waiting for some answers."

Judd was on his feet with a triumphant smile on his face. "I managed to locate a few rifle casings. Probably from the gun that shot Ray Hoy. Our killer may have been the same person with two different guns. I guess the trip out here was worthwhile. I'll have to take this jewelry bag to the lab for testing. Maybe we'll get a fingerprint too. Can we go back now?"

Bonnie and Matthew helped get the police boat back into the water before they left the island. She brought the smaller Wildlife boat close to the edge of the shore along the mainland as they searched for wolf prints that might show them the direction the wolves had gone to seek shelter from the fire and the snow.

Matthew finally pointed and drew her attention. "There they went. We can track them from there."

"Let's take the boat back to the dock and head this way on foot. If they're still close by, I don't want to scare them off."

They took their backpacks when they moored the boat and headed along the shore until they picked up the tracks again.

"Looks like they're headed east further into the mountains," Bonnie said.

"I think so. There are plenty of caves up there to shelter in," he replied. "Or they may just have run until they weren't afraid anymore."

They walked together, mindful of the tracks they followed. The wolves weren't the only animals fleeing from the fire and the storm. Hundreds of smaller animals—foxes, raccoons, rabbits—ran alongside them, looking for a safe place.

There was one track that was larger and particularly troubling amid the hundreds of others.

"What was a bear doing out here?" Matthew stopped to outline the big paw print with his finger. "They should be all tucked in for the winter by now."

Bonnie agreed. "Maybe there's a cave out there or it was sleeping in a big stump until the fire." She looked at the direction the bear prints took at one noticeable fork in the track. "I don't think it's looking for a cave now. I think it's headed toward food."

## Chapter Eighteen

They had to veer away from tracking the wolves. They wouldn't present a danger to the surrounding community, especially since there was only one adult and one pup according to their prints. But a hungry bear awakened from its hibernation too soon could cause a safety issue for the people who lived in houses nearby. It was part of her job to keep that from happening.

Bonnie had a tranquilizer pistol in her backpack, though it wouldn't be her first choice to use against the bear. Sometimes they could be diverted from the trashcans they smelled by a better meal.

"There are cabins up here," Matthew said. "They're probably empty right now. It's too early for ski season and too late for tubing in the river. The bear is probably headed there."

"We better get moving. Some people panic when faced with a bear."

He laughed. "You think? But not you, though, right? You just talk it down, and it goes away."

"I'm really not able to communicate with animals." She pushed her hair out of her eyes. "Let's just move on from the whole white fawn thing."

"We'll see."

A shotgun blast sent them running through the woods. Bonnie could see the beginning of some housing that faced the lake. Some of the houses were huge to just sit empty most of the year. They were beautiful too, with tall windows mirroring the water. Some of them looked like ski chalets and others like elegant cabins.

"I see him." Bonnie pointed to the man in his backyard facing an angry, hungry bear. "Oh no. The only thing worse than a bear with cubs is a pregnant bear. We can't tranquilize her, or she could lose the cubs."

"How can you tell she's pregnant from way back here? Is there a plan behind all that?" Matthew asked as he ran. "Because all I see is an angry frightened man who's going to shoot mama bear unless she attacks him first."

"Don't worry. We had bears in Alabama too. You just have to respect them. She really doesn't want to hurt him. She's just super hungry and cranky."

"Maybe so, but I don't think Mr. Homeowner feels the same way."

"Stop!" Bonnie called out as the man in his white T-shirt, shorts, and boots leveled his shotgun at the snarling bear. "I'm with the Wildlife Agency. Don't shoot that bear."

"You'd better get it out of my yard if you don't want me to kill it," the man yelled back.

But as he aimed the shotgun at the bear, she lifted one large paw and swiped at him, knocking the gun out of his hand and him to the ground. She loomed over him, growling and showing her teeth.

"Now's the time for that plan," Matthew suggested.

She didn't take out the pistol or touch the gun or taser at her belt. Instead she ran right up to the bear and put herself between the bear and the man on the ground. "This isn't a good idea. Not if you want to have those cubs. Even if you kill this man, more will come, and one of them will kill you."

The bear stopped snarling and stared at Bonnie.

"That's right," she encouraged. "Let's not even look at him. I've got some snacks in my backpack. Let's eat those instead, and then we'll find you something big to eat that's not human."

The bear made sounds at her like she was trying to talk back. It came out as a series of groans and bellows but no snarls or growling.

Bonnie put two power bars on the ground beside the bear so she had to turn away from the man she'd knocked down and possibly had planned to snack on. The bear grabbed both of them and put them in her mouth. They were barely noticeable in that wide, red cavity. But it was enough time for Matthew to get the other man off the frozen ground and headed toward his home.

"I need some food," she told him. "See if that man has anything she can eat."

"Yes ma'am." He ran to follow the man he'd just rescued. "Hey, wait. I need some food. Have you got some chicken or a nice ham?"

The bear dropped to all fours, but her eyes stayed

locked on Bonnie's. The two stood watching each other until Matthew came running out of the house with a whole roasted chicken.

Bonnie watched as the bear started to lunge toward the smell of food and the man carrying it. "Wait a minute. He's bringing it right here to you. Let's not eat the delivery driver."

Very carefully, Matthew approached them and slowly handed the chicken to Bonnie. "There's another one. I thought we could use that to lure her away from the area after she finishes this one."

"Here you go." She put the chicken on the ground where the power bars had been. "Of course you're hungry. Being pregnant takes a lot out of you. How can you sleep when you're hungry?"

The bear gobbled down the chicken and licked her lips. She made more guttural noises at Bonnie and waved her large paws around in the air.

"Let's get out of here. That way." She pointed. "Toward the mountains over there behind the lake. You should be able to sleep there for the winter without anyone bothering you again. And when you wake up next spring, there will be babies for you to feed and play with. It's gonna be okay. Just come with us."

"I'll get the other chicken," Matthew volunteered. "She doesn't want to follow me anyway. Look at her. She'd follow you whether you had food to eat or not, Unega Awinita. You still haven't proven me wrong."

Bonnie didn't have time to argue. The bear was loping along beside her as she started walking away from the expensive lake housing. She didn't think Matthew was right about her having any special powers. The bear was going with her because she'd fed her. She knew she'd better have something else for her to eat by the end of their journey, or she could just as easily turn on her.

It was a long hike. They got around the side of the lake and began the steeper ascent into the rugged terrain. There was the occasional path that they could discern, but mostly it was just them out there in the middle of miles of trees. Bonnie glanced at her watch. She wasn't going to make it home for lunch. She tried to call her mother but couldn't get enough signal on her cell phone.

Instead she called the police department on her radio and got rerouted to Officer Trump's police car. She told him her dilemma, and he promised to stop in to check on her mother. Bonnie thanked him and kept moving along with the bear.

A little after two p.m., they reached a creek that was full of water from the melting snow and ice. Bonnie paused for a moment and splashed some of the cold, clear water in her face.

The bear lifted her head after taking a deep drink and sniffed the air. She bellowed and began to take off in another direction further into the forest and away from Sweet Pepper. There seemed to be no stopping her as she recognized a previous dwelling and headed for it.

"You forgot your chicken," Matthew called out after her. "Oh well. I'm starving. I think it's time for lunch." He dropped to a large rock at the side of the creek. "Chicken?"

They stayed there eating and talking for about thirty minutes. Matthew looked around at their location and thought there was a faster way back to civilization from where they were. "It looks like we're a lot further from

Sweet Pepper than we are. We could've been up here an hour ago."

"The bear didn't exactly bring a map with her." Bonnie washed the chicken from her hands in the creek water. "But we got her up here, and she didn't try to eat either of us."

"No wonder. She knew you were on her side."

"Please. She knew I fed her so she was willing to put up with me."

"Has no one else ever noticed this about you? You worked with animals for the last ten years and no one thought your methods were insane?" He stared into her eyes until she looked away.

"I spent a lot of time by myself. But I've never had anyone make such a fuss over what I do."

"Are the people in Alabama crazy and blind? Or do they all talk to animals?"

Bonnie got up from the sunny rock where she'd been sitting. "The people in Alabama were friendly and wonderful. I hated to leave them."

"Oh yeah?" He glanced up at her. "Anyone in particular? Maybe they were afraid of you. Otherwise I think you would've brought someone back with you. No love interest?"

"Not that it's any of your business, but there was someone. It just didn't work out."

Matthew stood up close beside her. "We're working together. That makes it my business. And you can ask me anything about my personal life. You already know about my ex and my son. I was seeing a waitress over at Scooters Barbecue for a while, but that didn't work out either. Anything else you'd like to know?"

"Not really." But she smiled as she said it. "We

should get going. It's a long walk back, even with your shortcut."

"How can you say that? I haven't showed it to you yet." He pointed in the direction they needed to go and then turned his warm eyes back to her. "How about dinner Friday night—no kids and no relatives?"

"You don't waste any time, do you?"

"I can't afford to. I saw the way that wolf pup looked at you. I'm sure humans are probably affected by your charisma too. Ricky was flirting with you. Maybe John Trump too. It's good for people to know up front that you're with me."

She laughed as she followed him down the trail he claimed to be able to see. "That's the worst reason ever to go out on a date with someone."

"Oh sorry. Did you think I meant it was a date? No. This is just a friendship new working partner thing." He kept talking even though the terrain grew tougher with trees growing closer together.

"Really?" Had she misjudged his flirtations?

Matthew stopped and grinned when she walked right into him.

"No. Absolutely not. I just want to make sure no one else tried to date you." He put his big arms around her.

Her face was pushed into his chest—he was several inches taller than her. "You're very subtle."

"Subtle? Subtlety never got any man a girlfriend."

Bonnie put her arms between them. "Are we hiking out of here or what? I'd like to be back before dark."

"Sure. What did you have planned?"

"Okay, I'm taking point now." She disengaged herself from him and started walking again. Was he serious? It was hard to tell. Not that she wanted him to think of her romantically. They barely knew each other.

"See?" he asked from behind her. "Isn't this much better now that we both know how we feel?"

"I don't think either one of us feels any particular way about the other. Just keep walking."

"You walk. I'll follow. Try not to fall into the lake when we come to that sharp drop-off just beyond those trees. Not that I wouldn't enjoy a little mouth to mouth with you, Bonnie, but not after you were drowning."

She laughed at him again and kept walking. The trees were so tightly bunched together that it slowed their progress. Then suddenly the trees were gone, and her next step would have taken her over the edge of a sharp, twenty-foot drop into the cold lake.

Matthew immediately wrapped one arm around her waist and pulled her back from the edge. "You thought I was joking, didn't you?"

Bonnie wasn't close enough to the edge that she was worried about falling. She hadn't lived here in a long time, but she knew there were some scary and dangerous spots around the lake. She'd hiked these mountains since she was a teenager.

"I wasn't that close to the edge," she told him. "And we should maintain a professional relationship if we're going to work together. But thanks for your help."

He was right about the way back. It took a lot less time to reach the truck than it had taken to get above the lake. Of course they weren't shepherding a mother bear on the way down either.

They got in the truck and drove back to Sweet Pepper. Bonnie was hoping the impound lot was still open since it was after three p.m. She had no idea how long it stayed open.

There were carolers dressed in costumes from the 1800s walking along the sidewalks, singing Christmas songs at the top of their lungs. A church bell rang in the distance, and a sleigh with one horse was parked in front of town hall. The sleigh and the horse were decorated with flowers. The horse even wore a Santa hat.

"Christmas in Sweet Pepper," Matthew sighed as they passed the town lit by twinkle lights. "Almost as good as Christmas Eve in the valley."

"Are they doing something for Christmas in the valley now?" she asked. "They never did anything besides selling trees when I lived here."

"It's different now. Christmas Eve is the official end of the tree-selling season. There's a parade and Santa. People throw candy in the streets, and music plays until midnight to celebrate Christmas Day. Everyone has pancakes and sausages at the general store. And then we go home."

"Sounds exciting," she remarked as they stopped at the gate to the impound lot. "I'm here to get the Hummer," she told the man at the tiny guard house.

"Could I see some ID on that?" he asked, holding a clipboard. Dozens of sets of keys were lined up on the wall in the shack.

"Really, Sparky?" Matthew glanced around Bonnie's head. "Are you really asking me for ID?"

"Well, no. Not if it's you. I didn't see you in there. It's getting dark."

Bonnie held out her ID. "You're releasing the vehicle to me anyway."

"Oh, sure, Agent Tuttle." Sparky grinned and handed her the keys. "Chief said to give you a message too. He's got something going on at the police station.

He'd like it if you'd go there when you're done here."

"Thanks. I will."

It wasn't hard to find the Hummer in the dimly lit parking lot. It was the biggest thing there. Bonnie left her keys in the truck and got out.

"Don't you want me to drive the Hummer?" Matthew asked as he got out too.

"I told you—we can't do that. Regulations."

"Don't you ever break any regulations?"

"Not so you can drive the Hummer," she retorted. "Be careful with my brother's truck. Thanks for your help."

"Okay. But I feel so used, you know? You just push me aside, even though I saved your life today."

"Dream on." She waved as she got into the Hummer. Despite the fact that Matthew Brown Elk was a little crazy, they'd worked well together that day. She had to remember to put in a pay voucher for him and have him put on her regular contractor's list.

The Hummer drove like a tank. She wasn't surprised but was glad she'd driven every kind of truck and farm equipment in the past ten years. The vehicle seemed so out of place in quaint little Sweet Pepper. It took up two parking places in front of town hall.

Still, it would be helpful during the winter when the roads could be impassable. There was probably nothing—including a tree down in front of her—that it wouldn't go through or over.

Chief Rogers was waiting inside for her. She grabbed a cup of coffee and a blueberry muffin before she sat down with him. She was exhausted, hungry, and thirsty. This would tide her over until she could get home for supper.

"Where have you been all day?" He sat opposite her at his big desk. "You didn't answer your cell phone, but you managed to get a message out to Trump about your mother."

She described her day for him from the time they'd parted company at the island. "The important thing was we managed to get the bear away from the houses. I think she'll sleep peacefully now."

"Good work. I'd rather you took care of those calls than us." He smiled. "I have good news on another front. Judd identified a fingerprint on the red jeweler's bag you found out there. We didn't have to look far. It belongs to Vince Stookey. He's still not talking. The one thing he says is that he didn't kill Ray Hoy or Harvey. But I think we've got him."

"Did he say what happened to the ruby?"

"No. He says he didn't know anything about it. But I think we have enough to file with the DA. We'll see. But I've charged him with both murders, one count of B and E, and whatever the charge is for stealing Harvey's body."

"That's good news," she said, though it seemed to her that the evidence was flimsy. "Thanks, Chief. I'll sleep better tonight knowing that."

## Chapter Nineteen

But Bonnie didn't have the restful night she'd envisioned.

Everything was fine at the house. Her mother had made lunch for John Trump when he checked on her. She'd also had dinner waiting in the oven for Bonnie when she got back. Rose had gone to church, where they were working on wreaths for the Christmas Eve celebration. She'd left a note with the food and said she'd be back around ten.

The little wolf wasn't in his kennel, but she'd come to expect that. He was sleeping peacefully on her bed. Bonnie would believe that her mother was letting him out because she felt sorry for him, except that she had the key to the lock on her keyring. She lured him back to his kennel with some chicken. He was looking healthy and strong but might have a few scars on his back from the fire. His fur was already growing over the spot where the bullet had hit him.

"Listen, you," she said. "Matthew says animals understand me. If you do—stay off my bed. It's starting to smell wolfy in there. I couldn't find your mother, but we have a good idea where she is. It won't be long, and I'll take you up there to be with her."

He whined and lay down in the kennel without eating the chicken. His eyes stayed fixed on her.

"I told you that you can't stay. Trust me, you won't want to when you get bigger. There's a whole world out there for you. Goodnight. See you tomorrow. But not on my bed."

Bonnie latched the kennel but didn't bother to lock it. She went out and moved her brother's truck to the side of the house. She might use it for shopping if her truck was too expensive to repair. The Hummer was her work vehicle now. She missed her little Jeep that she'd used in Alabama.

After that, she finished going through all the papers and files she and Matthew had taken from Harvey's old office that morning. She smiled, thinking about him as she read the papers. It was hard to say if he always acted that way with a new woman or if he was seriously flirting with her. Maybe it was being out of the town that had done it. Only time and getting to know him better would say.

In the meantime, it had kind of cheered her up and helped her forget about Saul. She'd thought he might call when he found out she was gone. He still had her number. He was probably off somewhere helping his niece, Zoe, with her food truck business. It hadn't been his niece that caused Bonnie to believe she and Saul had no future. It was Saul himself and his reluctance to make anything permanent. He had a better relationship with his albino alligator than he had with most humans.

It was better not to think about it that way, she chided herself as she got up to add wood to the fire and get a fresh cup of hot cocoa. She was mixing the drink when someone knocked at her door. The little wolf howled as she went to answer it. Yes, he was definitely going to have to live in the wild again.

"Hi, Agent Tuttle." It was Jean Shelton.

"Mrs. Shelton, please come in. What can I do for you?"

"I hope I'm not disturbing you." Harvey's wife came in the foyer and looked around. "I was just thinking about a few things and wondering if you might be able to answer some questions for me."

"I'll try. Have a seat."

"I know you mentioned something about a ruby that Harvey found that he may have been killed for." Mrs. Shelton twisted her hands in her lap.

"That's right. Would you like something to drink? I have coffee, tea, and hot chocolate."

"No. Thanks anyway." Mrs. Shelton stared at Bonnie, her eyes still red from crying. "We have a financial crisis, Agent Tuttle. It seems my husband cashed in his retirement to put money down on the beach house. I'm assuming, though he never said a word to me about it, that he planned to sell this ruby to pay for it and replenish his account. So now I have no money, and Chief Rogers has told me he can't find the ruby."

"I'm so sorry," Bonnie said. "Maybe the finance company will let you get his retirement savings back if you release the beach house."

"They don't sound very flexible about it. In fact, they

are threatening to sue me for the rest of what is owed on the beach house. I'm not sure what to do about it. You know what the job pays. We don't have that kind of money."

Bonnie studied her, wondering why she'd come to her with the problem. She had to know that the Tuttles didn't have anything to lend her to help with the problem. "What can I do to help?"

"I need that ruby. My husband didn't steal it as far as anyone knows. That means it belongs to me now. I need to sell it and make everything right."

"Of course. I understand." Bonnie frowned. "But I really have no idea where it is. We've checked all over. It may be with whoever killed your husband."

"I've been afraid of that, and I've been thinking. Would it help if I offered a finder's fee? Chief Rogers said the ruby might be worth millions. If it would incentivize someone to come forward, it would be worth it."

"Maybe that would help," Bonnie replied, not really sure about that. If someone had the ruby, why not just sell it and take it all?

"Would it help you?" Mrs. Shelton's look was coy.

"No, ma'am. I'm looking as hard as I can for Harvey's killer but not for the ruby. You're welcome to try what you can to locate it. Please be sure to notify the police department if someone comes forward."

"I will." Mrs. Shelton got to her feet. "I hope you'll do the same and keep me in your thoughts as you search. Of course I want the killer as badly as you, but we could lose everything if the ruby isn't found."

Bonnie stood, inches over Mrs. Shelton even with her shoes off. "I'll do the best I can for you. Good luck, ma'am."

When the other woman was gone, Bonnie thought about the predicament Harvey's good fortune had put them in. There was really nothing she could do to help, but she felt bad for them. It hurt her professional pride that Mrs. Shelton thought she would do a better job if she offered her a financial reward, but it didn't really surprise her.

Rose got home a little after ten, filled with stories about working on the wreaths. Bonnie told her a condensed version of her day, and the two went to bed. The little wolf didn't howl when her mother came in the house, as he had when Mrs. Shelton had shown up. It was easy to compare him to a dog, but she knew that was a mistake. Wild animals were always wild.

They went to bed soon after, but Bonnie couldn't sleep. She'd already talked to her mother about using the office her father and brother had used in the house, and now she found herself in that room straightening up and boxing her brother's personal belongings so she'd have room for her own.

She remembered being in here plenty of times as a child when her father worked on what he planned to do to make the Christmas tree farm more productive. He and Eric had huge files in great detail on planting, fertilizing, and cutting. Neither one of them had been full-time tree farmers, even though it seemed like it from the amount of work they'd put into it. Bonnie hoped she was up to the task of working on the trees and keeping up with her work as a Wildlife Agent. She wasn't happy with the idea of giving up either effort, but she couldn't envision not doing her job with animals and humans that required so much of her.

By midnight, she felt settled into the office. She put up a few of Harvey's maps of the area they served. It was a huge territory, encompassing most of Tennessee and even part of North Carolina, which included the Cherokee Reservation. She'd have to plan some time to meet with the Cherokee tribal council soon. It was just another addition to a long list of settling into her job.

She checked the maps against known mineral areas that included rivers and streams where Harvey might have found his ruby.

"Not that it especially matters," she said aloud. "But where did you find it?"

Maybe it was better not to know. She'd have to include it in a report, and when that leaked out as it always seemed to do, that river or stream would be inundated with miners hoping to match Harvey's big score.

Bonnie heard a noise at the window and looked up to find Dustu coming in the house through the large pane. The little wolf was at his feet as he warmed his hands near the fire in the hearth.

"How did you get in here?" she asked the shaman. "What do you want?"

"I'm here to help you, as is your wolf." He smiled broadly. "Remember that you don't need to find the ruby. You need to find the killer, or he could kill again. He seeks the ruby and doesn't care how he comes by it. Protect yourself, Unega Awinita. You are more valuable than this thing he seeks."

The little wolf grinned too and wagged his tail.

"I think you should leave," she told the shaman and then turned to the wolf. "And you should get back in your kennel."

The wolf howled loudly and woke her up. She'd been asleep with her face on the desk, drooling a little on the wood. She wiped it up quickly and went to check on the wolf. He wasn't in his kennel, and she found him asleep on her bed again.

Before she could walk him back to his kennel and demand that he stay there, there was a loud knock on the front door. She was still in the clothes she'd slept in but ran her hand through her hair and went to answer.

It was a man with two children who wanted a Christmas tree. They didn't really open until nine a.m., but she remembered her father opening whenever he needed to and invited them in for a warm drink while she put on her boots and jacket.

Rose got up and made steaming bowls of oatmeal with raisins and brown sugar. The man was from Frog Pond. His wife was a nurse who was working the morning shift at the hospital in Sevierville. He wanted to surprise her when she came home by having the Christmas tree up in the living room. His two little girls were loud and full of energy. They ran ahead in the snow after breakfast as they argued about which tree was the perfect one.

The three hawks that had been on the hood of the truck yesterday called to Bonnie from the roof of the barn, as if demonstrating that the one she'd tended was all right. She nodded to them as she picked up a chainsaw and headed to the tree the girls had chosen.

The tree was cut and bundled by nine a.m. and then tied to the top of the car. She waved goodbye to the family, who'd paid well for their tree. The money had made up for what she'd lost the day before. Had this been the way it was for Eric and her father? She'd have to remember to ask him when he came back for Christmas.

The pepper factory foreman called about an injured deer that had been found in the parking lot. Bonnie promised to be there as soon as she could—which included time to shower and change clothes. The wolf had gone back into the kennel without her help this time. It seemed pointless to bother closing the door since he came and went as he pleased. She gave him some chicken and wondered how he and the shaman had managed to get into her dreams.

"I think I'm getting too close to you too, little man." She reached a hand to stroke his coat. He looked up but ignored her as she touched him. "No. This can't happen. I have to find you a home."

Bonnie told Rose she'd be back for lunch and went out to the Hummer. There were no injured animals and no sign of Matthew. She was alone to work as she chose, as she'd been most of the time in Alabama. The Hummer was loud as she started it, but she'd get used to it. She'd get used to all of this as part of her new life.

Life had made her a pragmatic woman. She'd made one big mistake early on that had cost her dearly. Recovering from that had meant being more careful than most people—she looked more than once before she took a step, much less a leap. None of that had changed since she got home. The shaman in her dream was probably nothing more than her own subconscious warning her to be careful.

That was one thing no one had to warn her about.

The pepper plant on the high hill overlooking Sweet Pepper was at full shift that morning. With the ice and snow completely gone, the factory the town had been built around was humming along. Bonnie had called ahead and the plant manager met her in the parking lot.

"She's back here." The plant manager walked her around to the area where trucks would normally be parked to take the hottest, sweetest peppers in the world to market. "The men who found her just wanted to put her out of her misery."

"I'm glad you stopped them," she said.

"I told them there was a stiff penalty for shooting a doe out of season," he continued. "I won't have that going against the pepper plant. What you do from here is up to you, Agent Tuttle."

He walked away without offering any other assistance. Bonnie revised her initial impression of him. He wasn't interested in helping the doe. He just wanted her off the property in the least troublesome manner.

"Okay." She knelt on the cold blacktop and stroked the doe's head. "Looks like you got hit by something. I'm guessing you can't get up."

The doe made a snorting sound and moved her head, her large, brown eyes staring into Bonnie's in fear and pain.

"Let's see where the problem is and what we can do to get you out of here."

Bonnie checked the doe's front legs—they seemed to be fine—and then her back legs. Her left back leg seemed to be broken, her hoof bent at a strange angle. When she touched it, the doe started up trying to get away. Bonnie soothed her and convinced her to stay where she was.

She realized she was going to have to move her, but it was at least a two person job. It would've been better if Matthew had been there, but she was used to figuring these things out on her own.

Going back to the Hummer, she backed the vehicle until it was close to the doe. She assured the doe again that she'd be fine but her injury needed more than Bonnie could provide at the scene.

"Don't worry," she told the doe as she took out the large, heavy harness. It was attached to a winch that could raise and lower heavy animals. "Let's just get this around you, and we'll have you up in the back in no time. We're going to have to find that vet that takes care of wild animals. But you're going to be fine."

The doe gave her a skeptical look. Bonnie wished she really could speak to animals. She could reassure the doe of everything she was saying.

Bonnie got the harness on the doe and kept her hand on the doe's neck as the winch pulled the harness up. She gently pushed the harness toward the back of the hummer and lowered the doe inside. She was pleased when the animal was safely in the vehicle and glad she had the harness and winch to work with. Sometimes she had one in Alabama, and sometimes she had to share it with others.

"All right. This is going to be loud and bumpy, but everything will be better once we get to the vet. Trust me, you're going to be fine."

The doe made bleating noises of protest and tried to get up. But after a few minutes, she lay down her head and was quiet.

With the back door closed and the doe secure, she drove to the far edge of the parking lot so she wouldn't be in the way of vehicles going in and out. She looked up the phone number she'd been given to contact the wildlife vet in Sevierville. She had to leave a message, of course. The only address was a post office box number, so she couldn't just GPS the vet and find him by herself.

That meant waiting for a return call.

"I'm sorry," she told the doe. "But at least you're not on the cold parking lot ground. We'll just have to wait until we hear back."

Waiting was hard when she knew the doe was hurt. She left two more messages for the vet, including one where she gave him instructions on how to find her. That would save some time if he decided to come out this way.

She didn't hear anything back from the vet and kept calling. During one call she glanced out the side window and looked at the old ice house. The door was wide open. Someone was careless. Maybe they'd shut it off. If not, it was cooling all of Sweet Pepper. It probably didn't matter since the temperature in the ice house was about the same as it was outside the ice house.

Still, she had some time on her hands. She promised the doe that she'd be right back and went to check on the situation.

The door was open because the lock had been cut off. The tables where they'd kept Harvey and Ray Hoy had been tossed aside. It looked as though someone had vandalized the place. It wasn't hard to guess what they were searching for. By now, word of the missing ruby would have been all over town. She could see where it would be a sensible place to look for it if the police hadn't already extensively searched.

She turned to walk out of the ice house and heard a sound before it felt like the back of her head exploded and she fell to the floor.

## Chapter Twenty

The next thing Bonnie knew, someone was calling her name. She opened her eyes and saw three pairs of eyes looking back at her. Her head was pounding, and she felt like she was going to throw up.

"What happened?" She put one hand to the back of her head and tried to sit up.

"Not so fast," one of the men, a stranger, advised.

"Someone hit you in the head," John Trump said. "D.W. called when he found you here on the floor."

"D.W.?" Bonnie asked.

"You called me about the doe, remember? D.W. Vance." The older man with the huge, gray beard reminded her. "Sit still a minute. Let me take a look at your head."

"Uh…you're a vet," Matthew reminded him. "She's a person. You should go tend to the deer. John, call an ambulance."

"I'm okay." Bonnie shrugged off all three of them and got to her feet. She was woozy but didn't fall over again. "Why would someone hit me in the head?"

"Probably looking for the ruby," John said. "Looks like they worked this place over."

"I guess that means the killer must still be on the loose and trying to find the ruby," Matthew added.

"What ruby?" D.W. asked as he felt around on the back of Bonnie's skull. "I don't feel a fracture, and you're not bleeding. They just hit you hard enough to knock you out. You have a low threshold of consciousness, most likely, and uh…you might want to button up there. And your pockets are pulled out. I think someone worked you over too, Agent Tuttle."

He fastened the buttons left open on her shirt, and she pushed in her pockets. Her cell phone and radio were still on her, along with her gun and Taser.

"What do you want me to do with the doe?" D.W. asked.

Bonnie wanted to sit down but was afraid she wouldn't make it to the Hummer. She stood still instead and waited for the dizziness to pass. Coffee and an aspirin would be good about then. "I think she has a broken leg. Can you treat her?"

He nodded, his long, blondish gray hair swinging into his face. "Sure. I can treat her. Can you pay?"

"I can." She nodded, stopping abruptly when her head felt like it was going to fall off. "Or rather, I can put in a voucher with the Wildlife Agency so you get paid."

His bright blue eyes lingered on her face. "You're new here. You can't save every animal that gets hit by a car, shot by a gun or an arrow, or all the other things that happen. The agency won't pay for it, and then you and I would have a problem."

"Maybe this isn't the best time to negotiate that deal," John said. "Grab my keys, Brown Elk. I'll take Bonnie in the Hummer."

"You can't drive the Hummer," Matthew told him. "Only someone who works for the feds can do that. Ask her if you don't believe me."

"This is an emergency," John replied. "And I'm an officer of the law, not to mention that she'll be in the vehicle. I'm taking her back to town hall to fill out a police report."

"All right." Matthew took John's keys and went to the police car.

"I'll make an exception with the doe this time," D.W. told Bonnie. "You fellas help me move the deer to my pickup. Give me a call later, Agent. We'll talk then."

It was all a little foggy for Bonnie. She could barely remember getting in the Hummer and ending up at town hall. She woke up again lying on a worn sofa in the police breakroom with several officers staring at her.

"Good morning, sunshine," Officer Skeet Richardson said with a cup of coffee in one hand and a donut in the other. "How's that head doing?"

"They should have taken her to the hospital," Officer Nancy Bradford said. "Don't we even get medical attention anymore?"

"I'm fine," Bonnie said. "Thanks. I could really use some coffee and an aspirin."

"Help yourself," Skeet said and then mindful of her injury, got aspirin, coffee, and a donut for her. "You sure you're feeling okay?"

"I'm sure. Thank you."

He stepped into the hall outside the breakroom and

told John that she was awake.

"You look better." John summed up her appearance. "Are you up to a debriefing with Chief Rogers?"

She nodded and her head hurt but didn't feel as though she might lose it. "His office?"

"Conference room. The coroner is here too."

John led the way. Judd Streeter and Chief Rogers were waiting in the conference room with Stella and another man that Bonnie didn't recognize.

"How are you?" Stella asked. "John tells me you have a hard head like me too."

"I guess so." Bonnie found a place to sit and waited. Stella introduced her to Rufus Palcomb. They'd spoken on the radio but hadn't met yet.

"Looks like we've got some good news and some bad news," Chief Rogers began the conversation as everyone took a seat around the table. "First off, we had to let our only suspect go this morning. We checked his .38 against the bullet taken from Harvey Shelton, and it wasn't a match. That, and the attack on Agent Tuttle tells us we're on the wrong track. His lawyer took him home after getting the breaking and entering charge against him reduced by the DA."

"What's the good news?" Stella asked.

"The good news sounds a lot like the bad news," the chief said. "Because Agent Tuttle was clearly attacked by someone looking for the ruby, we know the killer is still out there and hasn't managed to find and sell it."

Judd cleared his throat and laughed. "It seems I have the best news of all—despite the fact that Chief Rogers upstaged me by giving you forensic information."

The chief nodded. "Sorry, Judd."

"That's quite all right."

They all waited as the coroner produced a plastic bag that contained the red velvet bag they believed Harvey had used to carry the ruby around with him.

"I was puzzling over how the ruby could be missing from the jeweler's bag and yet no one seemed to have the stone. I thought a lot about this one and went back to the body for evidence. There it was." He paused for effect until he brought out another evidence bag that held a large red gemstone. "And here it is."

Everyone around the table marveled at the size of the pigeon-blood ruby. It was beautiful, raw and uncut, a stone worth dying for.

"How did you miss it the first time?" Chief Rogers asked. "And where did you find it? We thoroughly searched his clothes."

"It was lodged in his esophagus." Judd held the stone up to the light. "I believe Harvey thought he could swallow it and keep his killer from getting it. He died before it could get to his stomach, which was why I didn't find it the first time around."

John Trump sat back in his chair with a sigh. "That just makes it harder to catch the killer. We were hoping we could get him when he tried to sell the stone. That can't happen now."

They all agreed with that. Suggestions flew fast and furiously around the table, but nothing more really came of the meeting. Stella and Rufus, the pilot of the *Tennessee Teardrop* fireboat, couldn't recall seeing a particularly strange boat at the fire since there were so many boats.

"It wasn't just our boats or police boats," Stella said. "There were dozens of boats with people who just wanted to see what was going on. If any of them was the killer, my people were too busy with the fire to look around to see if there was a rifle."

Chief Rogers nodded. "Like I said, good and bad news. We have no suspect, but we have the ruby. I spoke with Harvey's family. They didn't know anything about the stone or the beach house. I tend to believe them because the real estate people I spoke with only met with Harvey and the property was only in his name."

"So maybe he didn't even plan to take his family," Stella said.

"I don't know," the chief admitted. "Let's work on a strategy, people. I don't want the FBI in here investigating the death of a Federal Wildlife Agent—which they assuredly will be, unless we come up with something. Have you heard anything from the FBI or your superiors in Wildlife, Bonnie?"

"No, sir. But I've been out a lot with not much cell service," she admitted. "I can make some calls and see what's planned."

"Thanks, but let's not start a fire if we don't have a steak," Chief Rogers chuckled at his own humor. "All right, then. All of you keep me up to date on anything you find out."

The group began to leave the room. Stella stayed an extra moment to talk to Bonnie and make sure she was all right.

"I guess you didn't see anything," she said, with Rufus beside her on one side.

Bonnie wondered if Eric Gamlyn was on her other side. "No, the attack came from behind."

"This man must be desperate to attack you looking for the ruby," Rufus suggested. "Maybe there's some way to use that against him."

"Good idea, Palcomb," John said. "Come up with a plan to do it."

"I don't plan." Rufus grinned. "I'm leaving that to you. I don't even get paid to do my job."

Bonnie excused herself and found an empty desk where she could call D.W. Vance and find out about the doe. His phone went right to an answering machine again. She left a message then started thinking about going home for the rest of the day. There wasn't much else she could do, and she still felt like someone had hit her in the head and left her lying on a cold stone floor—which they had.

Stella and the others were going for lunch at the cafe. They asked Bonnie if she wanted to go with them. She turned them down and left town hall.

Matthew was waiting by the Hummer when she got outside. "So is everything resolved?"

"No. Everything is a mess still. No answers. Just a lot of questions."

"I think I found your little wolf's mama and sister. After you ditched me this morning, I had some time to look around where we'd left off by the lake. I found their den. I thought you might want to know—and I'm charging you for the time."

"I didn't ditch you. We don't always need to work together."

"Whatever."

The weather was beautiful with a clear, sunny sky and mild temperatures forecast for the next few days. It was as good a time as any for her to reintroduce the wolf pup into the wild. If she waited too long, he would never reintegrate with his family.

"I'll take him there this afternoon. Thanks for

checking it out."

"You should let me take him. I don't think he'll stay up there anyway—he belongs to you. But if it is going to work to give him back to his family, he needs someone to do it that he doesn't care about. That sounds like me."

"I'm surprised you're offering," she said. "Why even bother trying if you don't think he'll stay?"

"Because sometimes I'm wrong." He smiled. "And you could use the afternoon off. But only if I can drive the Hummer."

Bonnie checked the rules, and as long as Matthew was her contractor, he could drive the Hummer. They drove back to the valley, and she gave him the keys. Her head hurt, and her stomach didn't feel so good either. She spoke briefly to her mother and went to bed.

She couldn't believe when she woke up again that it was six-thirty p.m. It was dark outside, and her mother was making supper in the kitchen. She'd lost a whole day thanks to whoever had attacked her.

But her headache was gone, and she was hungry. She just had to let it go and move on. When they finally caught whoever killed Harvey, she'd give him a thump on the head.

Bonnie shuffled into the kitchen and poured herself a cup of coffee.

"There you are. I was wondering if you were ever going to wake up," Rose said. "I have some stew with rosemary in it, just the way you like it."

"Thanks, Mom. Did Matthew come back after he dropped off the wolf?"

"He did. He left the keys and said he'd taken care of it. I guess you had to put the little wolf back with his family. Too bad. I enjoyed having him around."

"And that's why you kept letting him out of his kennel?"

"I never let him out. I thought you did it."

"I guess it doesn't matter anymore. He's gone." Bonnie smiled and sipped her coffee.

They ate stew and cornbread for supper. Bonnie went out afterward for an evening Christmas tree sale. Her father had installed lights in the field to see the trees and the wrapping machine. It was fun going out in the dark, walking through the trees with the crunch of snow under her boots.

After the six-foot blue spruce was mounted on the roof of the customer's car, she turned off the lights and stared at the moon glinting off the snow. The temperature had dropped, and the wind whistled down from the mountains. Her breath turned to frost, and her fingertips were cold. But it was a beautiful night. The stars were so clear that she could pick out all the constellations she knew, most of them what her father had taught her.

She'd missed this in the heart of Alabama. That cold clarity that came in the winter brought long thoughts of where she'd go and what she would do. It was much different than the wet heat and mosquitos.

The little shaman appeared on her way back to the house, riding the big stag. The moonlight didn't pass through him as she supposed it would a ghost. Thinking about Eric Gamlyn had made her wonder if Dustu was a ghost too.

"You survived," he exclaimed. "Congratulations. You were fortunate this time, but you did not heed my warning."

"I'm not sleeping," she said as much to him as to

herself. "I can't be dreaming."

"Did you think you were?"

"What do you want from me?"

"I want you to do all the things you were sent here to do, Unega Awinita. Nothing more. I am certain you will do well."

Not understanding what he was talking about, she watched him ride away between the trees again, but there was something left behind in the moonlight—the little wolf.

## Chapter Twenty-one

"Oh no. No. This isn't going to happen. How did you find your way back here anyway?"

He didn't move, just sat and watched her.

"Go home. Your mother and sister are looking for you. You can't live here."

He still didn't move. Bonnie decided she'd just ignore him and he'd leave.

"Hey." Matthew came through the snow toward her. "I saw your lights on and thought you might need some help."

"I do but not with the tree. Did you take him to the mountains?" She glanced at the wolf pup.

"You know I did." He laughed. "I told you that he doesn't belong to his family anymore. He belongs to you."

"You also told me I could talk to animals and they listened. I told him to leave. He's still here. It doesn't make a good case for your suppositions."

They started walking toward the house. The wolf followed them. Bonnie tried not to notice him, but it wasn't easy. He couldn't just stay out here in the cold by himself. He was too young to take care of himself. That should still have been his mother's job. But if she took him inside again, he might never leave.

"How are you feeling?" Matthew asked. "You were asleep when I got back."

"I'm better, thanks. And thank you for trying to take the wolf home. I think you may be wrong about that too. I think I need to take him to his den and tell him to stay there. That might work."

"Like I said, I'm not always right." He shrugged. "Are you going to the Christmas Eve festivities?"

"Probably. I haven't been in a long time, but I suppose I will since Mom is so involved with it."

"But you're not looking forward to it," he guessed. "It'll be fun. And I'd be happy to escort you and your mother."

"I don't know—"

"Or if you're not comfortable with that, then Peter, Thomas, and I could go with you and your mother. That way it will be less personal. We'd just be any other group."

Rose had already mentioned something similar, even though Eric would be back for the holiday. It wasn't like they needed men to go with them. But Rose liked the Brown Elk family and enjoyed little Peter's company.

"That's fine," she finally said after weighing all the options. She still wasn't sure that she'd go at all. Her encounter with Lindsey Blake had taught her that she was still raw about the subject, even though so much time had passed.

Her phone rang. It was Chief Rogers. "Sorry it's so late, Bonnie, but we just found Vince Stookey floating in the lake."

"What?" Matthew asked after she'd thanked the chief and said she'd be there as soon as possible.

"Now there are no real suspects," she said. "This case just keeps getting weirder. Maybe the FBI or Wildlife needs to come in and sort this out."

He convinced her to let him go with her, even though she assured him that she was driving. Bonnie had to leave her mom a note since Rose was already asleep when she looked in on her.

The little wolf sat on the front porch illuminated by a shaft of moonlight. She could only describe the look on his face as sad. It was ridiculous. He didn't feel sad because she was leaving. They'd worried too much about the wolf getting attached to her and not enough about her getting attached to the wolf.

On the way up the mountain, Bonnie told Matthew about seeing Dustu again. "I wish people would speak plainly. The only thing I understand when he talks is that he expects me to do something, but he doesn't make it clear what he expects."

"Thomas is involved with the tribal council. He told them about your encounter with Dustu. They weren't as excited as we were about it. He thinks they'd be just as happy not to see him again. It seems he's something of a troublemaker. Maybe you should be careful about doing anything he suggests."

"Great. I suppose he gave them my name too." She sighed. "I was hoping to attend their next meeting since the Wildlife Agency works with them. Now it won't be my reputation as an agent that goes with me—it will be my conversations with the shaman."

"Don't worry about it," he advised. "They'll probably forget about it. Can you put off a meeting with them for a year or so?"

She laughed as she tried to find a space by the lake to park. The parking lot was full of police cars and fire brigade vehicles. "I probably can't wait that long, but maybe something else will happen that takes their mind off of it."

"You know, you should smile more often. You look really sad most of the time. You're not old enough to be so sad. Not to mention that you've never been married." He grinned.

Chief Rogers knocked on the window. He stepped back as Bonnie opened the door. "I was wondering if you two were going to get out or if there was something going on in here that we all should share in."

"Just discussing the case, sir," she said. "Why is the fire brigade here? Was something on fire before you found Vince?"

"Nope. They like to show up for all emergencies. Chief Griffin wants them to get as much experience as they can since they're only volunteers."

Not that Bonnie minded Stella being there with her fire brigade crew of about ten people. She was just surprised.

"Lucky for us, Judd was still here in town. He's with the body now. Believe me, Sweet Pepper is never this crazy. I can't believe this is going on so close to the holiday. I don't know what's gotten into people."

"I'd say it was greed, Chief," Bonnie said. "A pretty,

red rock like that is bound to bring out the worst in people."

"Well at least you know for sure that Vince wasn't the killer," Matthew said. "Who is left?"

They walked together to the spot where Vince had been fished out of the lake. Judd Streeter confirmed that Vince was dead. "I don't see signs of any other trauma. I'll know more when I do the autopsy. Right now my preliminary conclusion is that he died of drowning."

"Thanks, Judd." Chief Rogers stared at Vince's face. It looked even more ghastly in the moonlight. "He might've drowned, but I guarantee he didn't push himself in."

"This feels like someone tying up loose ends," Bonnie said. "Harvey was killed because he couldn't keep his good fortune about finding that ruby to himself. I understand how men like Ray Hoy and Vince got involved in wanting to take it from him. But they didn't mastermind this, and now the real killer has gotten rid of his partners."

"And how are we supposed to smoke him out?" John Trump joined them, though he was dressed in a fire brigade bunker coat and boots.

"Good question," Chief Rogers agreed. "We have to think of something. I don't want this on my desk over the holidays. I'm going home for supper now, ladies and gents. Don't call until morning."

The fire brigade was packing up, and a truck had pulled up to take Vince's body to the morgue. Police officers directed traffic as dozens of cars and pickups left at the same time.

Bonnie glanced out her window as she waited to leave, admiring the moonlight on the water. "I guess I'm going to ask for help tomorrow morning. I think this might be more than Sweet Pepper can handle."

"You might as well sleep on it tonight," Matthew suggested. "Maybe Dustu will come and give you some clues."

"Even if he did, he'd say it so cryptically that I wouldn't know what he was talking about. But I don't think a protector of the woods and wildlife will have any idea how to solve this."

She dropped Matthew off at his house before swinging across the street into her driveway. She sat in the Hummer for a few minutes, looking at the moon and thinking about how life could quickly change from the way it usually was to something completely different.

It had happened for her with Davis as she'd joyfully shared her news about their child. She'd known before she stopped speaking that this wasn't what he wanted.

It had to be the same for Harvey as he looked into the eyes of the man who was willing to kill him for the ruby he'd been so excited about.

There were no doubt millions of such events every day that turned a person's life from happiness to sorrow or despair to hope. The problem was you just never knew when one of those moments was upon you.

Bonnie finally got out of the vehicle and went up the stairs to the door. The little wolf was sitting silently on the porch, not moving, just staring at her. How could she let him sleep outside by himself? She'd let him in for one more night and then take him up into the mountains to leave him with his family.

"Okay. Come on." She opened the front door. "Get inside. We'll talk about this tomorrow."

He ran in as she had the door open and jumped on

her bed.

"No. You can't sleep there. Let's go back to the laundry room. You don't have to sleep in the kennel, but you can't sleep in here."

Bonnie led him back to the laundry room. He sat in the middle of the floor, looking at her.

"Goodnight. Get some sleep. We have a big day coming up." She didn't dare look at his face.

She didn't have any problem sleeping. Her head hit the pillow, and she didn't wake up until morning. It was cloudy outside, with heavy clouds hanging on the mountains as though they were impaled there. But it was bright enough to see the wolf pup sleeping at the foot of the bed. Bonnie sighed, got up, and got ready to face the day.

"What are you doing?" her mother asked as Bonnie opened the kitchen door and the wolf pup ran outside. "I thought Matthew took him home yesterday?"

"He did, and the wolf came back last night. I couldn't leave him outside all night. He's not big enough to take care of himself against predators. I guess I'm putting him outside before he has an accident in here."

Rose smiled as she checked the waffle maker. "I knew you loved that little guy. I'm glad he's back."

"I'm taking him back up there again today—unless he wants to run away on his own right now. Wolves can't live with people. They're wild animals."

"And here I thought you knew all about wild animals. Wolves live with people sometimes. I saw a man on TV with one. And those magicians have tigers. It just all depends on the animal and the person. My cousin Fred had a pet raccoon for years until he was run over by a snowmobile."

Bonnie smiled as she got coffee for both of them. "The raccoon or Cousin Fred?"

"Sit down and eat your waffles," Rose said with a laugh. "I'm on my way to the church to get things ready for the live nativity. Nate Oswald is letting us use his chickens for it. I think live animals are very important to the whole thing. They used people but plastic animals last year. It just wasn't the same."

They ate their waffles together while Bonnie listened to her mother talk about how wonderful the Christmas Eve festivities were going to be. Rose was excited about the float she was riding on—the same one as Santa.

When they were done, they cleared the table, and Rose opened the door. "He didn't run away," she announced proudly. "I'm glad we still have some chicken left."

She fed the wolf and agreed to let Bonnie drop her off at the church since it was so cold that morning. They went out to the Hummer, and the wolf jumped inside as soon as the door was open. He settled down in the back, like he'd been doing it all his life. Rose laughed and raved about how smart he was.

Bonnie dropped her mother off at the church. She watched her hurry inside with dozens of other volunteers who made the Christmas Eve event special. As she was sitting there, Bonnie noticed something the investigators hadn't taken out of the Hummer when they were looking for clues.

It was only a medallion of some kind that Harvey had kept in there—probably a Saint Christopher medal—probably for luck. It hadn't helped him much, but as she stared at it, she thought about how far out of the way someone had taken Harvey's body to leave it in the Hummer by the lake. The ice house where it had been stolen was across town.

Why not just dump the body anywhere once it had been searched for the ruby? Why take him to the Hummer and leave him?

With the question came a moment of enlightenment. Whoever had taken Harvey's body cared about him. That person wanted him to be found so he could have a decent funeral. That person wasn't only interested in the ruby. He or she was also interested in Harvey.

She wasn't sure about the person who moved Harvey being the same person who'd killed him, but she knew where to start looking for the person who'd brought him back to the Hummer.

Mrs. Shelton.

Bonnie knew she needed to escort the wolf pup back into the mountains, but talking to Harvey's wife was more important. She started to back up out of the church parking lot when a hand opened the passenger door and Matthew jumped into the Hummer with her.

"What's up?" he asked. "Planning to ditch me again?"

## Chapter Twenty-two

"I didn't ditch you," she sputtered. "I can't take you everywhere with me."

"Why not? No one would've hit you on the head yesterday if I'd been there."

"I work alone."

"Maybe you shouldn't."

They stared at each other across the seat—Matthew serious and Bonnie irritated.

"Are you saying this because I'm a woman and you don't think I can handle the job?"

"No, I'm saying this because I always worked with Harvey except the day he was killed. If you don't believe me, check my pay vouchers. Harvey always wanted me there. It makes sense to have someone back you up."

"I understand." She nodded. "You feel guilty because Harvey was killed and then yesterday I was injured. But you weren't responsible for either event. I don't know if we can always work together."

He frowned. "Why not? We work well together. Did you have a problem with me being there? I think I saved your life at least once."

"I don't think you did." She sighed. "But we did work well together. I don't know. I'm not used to having a partner. Let me think about it."

Matthew crossed his arms over his chest. "Don't think too long, or you could lose me to another Federal Wildlife Agent. I'm in high demand, you know."

She laughed at him. "Considering the next Federal Wildlife Agent is in another state, I'm not going to worry about it." Her phone rang. It was D.W. Vance.

"Your doe is doing great. I'm keeping her today, but you can come get her tomorrow," he said with no polite hello or how are you.

"Okay. Wouldn't it be easier for you to just take her back and release her near the pepper factory?"

"I'm not driving all the way up there again. Come get her here, or she can wander off into Sevierville."

The phone went dead, and Bonnie stared at it. "What a rude, obnoxious man."

"Yeah," Matthew agreed. "But he's a good guy. Once you get to know him."

She hoped that was true since she'd possibly be seeing a lot of him. "All right. I'm going to talk with Harvey's widow again. I had an idea that came to me when I got in the Hummer this morning." She briefly explained.

He touched the medallion that she'd left on the console. "You had a vision. I'm sure it's meant to guide you to the truth since that's what you were looking for."

"After that I'll take Oginali home. We'll see after that

what comes up."

"Sounds good to me." He fastened his seat belt. "Wait. What did you call him? Are you talking about your wolf?"

She thought about what she'd said. "I don't know. I don't even know what that means. Maybe I heard it somewhere. I don't know why I said it."

"It's Cherokee for friend." He laughed heartily and hugged her. "You really did have a vision that named your wolf for you. Wow. That's exciting."

"I didn't have a vision. I'm sure I heard someone else say it, and it just sneaked into my conversation. I've never said Oginali before."

This time when she said the word, the little wolf jumped from the back of the vehicle to the console between her and Matthew. He didn't wag his tail like a dog but stared at her thoughtfully with great intensity in his eyes.

"You see? You called him." Matthew stroked the wolf's new fur. "Oginali. A good name for a companion."

The wolf turned to him and growled low, showing his teeth.

"Okay." Matthew took his hand away. "It's okay, little buddy. I mean you no harm. I work with your companion."

"Get in back," Bonnie said to the wolf without really thinking about it. The wolf complied but sat on the seat behind her staring earnestly at her. "This is hard to take in. I don't know what's going on, but the wolf and the deer will be better off with their families—after we see Mrs. Shelton."

"It's wonderful," Matthew exclaimed. "You truly

are Unega Awinita."

"If you keep calling me that, we're definitely not working together." She finished backing up and pulled out of the church parking lot.

"All right." He grinned. "I'll never call you that again. But it doesn't change what you are. It's an honor to work with you."

Bonnie wasn't happy with his response. But he was in the vehicle, and she was headed to a confrontation with a woman who may have killed her own husband. She needed to get her head in the game, and having Matthew there might prevent any further complications.

Mrs. Shelton answered the door with a smile that faded when she saw Bonnie and Matthew. "What do you want now? I don't think you should be here."

"I'm sorry you feel that way," Bonnie said. "But we have good news for you. I'm sure you'll want to hear it."

"Good news?" Mrs. Shelton was suspicious. "What kind of good news? Have you found Harvey's killer?"

"Better news than that for you, ma'am. It's about the ruby. May we come in? The wind is strong this morning."

"Of course." Mrs. Shelton had hesitated but finally opened the door wide. "Please hurry. My son and daughter are due back anytime. They wouldn't like you being here."

"It won't take long." Bonnie smiled to reassure her as she walked into the foyer.

Mrs. Shelton showed them to a small room with a fire burning in the hearth. Her eyes were alight with anticipation, and her lips trembled slightly. "What about the ruby? How big is it? Can I see it? I need to have it appraised."

Bonnie sat down. Matthew stood quietly by the fire. Mrs. Shelton sat beside Bonnie and leaned toward her.

"I don't have it with me, I'm afraid," she told Mrs. Shelton. "But I've seen it. It's very big. I'm not a jeweler, but I'm sure it's worth a fortune, just like Harvey said. It's in the custody lock-up with the police and will remain there until Harvey's killer is caught."

"What?" Mrs. Shelton was clearly shocked at knowing she still couldn't have the stone. "But we'll have nothing. Harvey's retirement is gone. This house belongs to the Wildlife Agency. And the beach house people..." She put her head in her hands and sobbed.

A vehicle came to a screeching halt outside, and a car door slammed.

Mrs. Shelton wiped away her tears and sat up straight again. "My children—"

Before she could finish, the front door flew open, and Gerald erupted into the room. Bonnie had never seen him like this before. His clothes and hair were dirty, and he had several days of stubble on his face. But the biggest difference was in his eyes—they looked feral. He glared at both women but didn't seem to see Matthew.

"Mother, what are doing talking to her?"

She stood up. "I told her to leave, that you'd be angry. She knows about the ruby. All about it. Do you know what this means?"

"What do you know?" Gerald demanded of Bonnie. His voice took on an edge of despair. "She gave it you, didn't she, Mother?"

"No. No, I don't have it." Mrs. Shelton cried, putting up her hands as if to show him.

"Now, Mr. Shelton, if you'll just calm—" Bonnie began in a soothing tone.

"The truth!" Gerald pulled a pistol from his jacket pocket, aiming at his mother. "My life depends on that stone!"

Through her tears, Mrs. Shelton whispered, "What is going on? No, I don't have it."

"Mr. Shelton." Bonnie stepped very slowly closer to Gerald. Matthew was still near the fireplace, completely unmoving. But his body was tensed to take action, and he nodded almost imperceptibly in her peripheral vision. She knew he was ready. "Your mother doesn't have the ruby."

"Then where is it? I need it!" Gerald glanced at Bonnie then Matthew. He held the gun towards his mother's head. Tears ran down his cheeks, but his hand was steady. "Tell me," he hissed. "And don't come near me. I'll kill her."

Bonnie had dealt with plenty of unreasonable people, but they were usually pointing their gun at an animal, not their own mother.

"Vince had it. I convinced him to turn it in to the cops," she lied, taking another step toward the gunman. "It's in the evidence room right now."

"Stand still!" Gerald yelled. "He didn't have the ruby. He couldn't have turned it in. He's dead."

"You can still stop this." She spoke evenly, despite the lump in her throat. Only the officials knew about Vince's death. She had to try to get him to give up the gun. "Why don't you put that down? Then we can talk about this."

"They are going to kill me if I don't hand over that rock." He shifted his aim toward Bonnie and cocked the gun. "You have to bring it to—"

The wolf pup howled in the doorway, loud and

long. The sound reverberated through the small house. Bonnie didn't have time to worry about how he'd gotten in here. She kept her gaze steady on the gun.

Gerald swung around, surprised, and fired toward the pup. "You should be dead! I already shot you!"

Matthew lunged at the crazed man, knocking him to the floor and pinning him down. The gun flew from Gerald's hands, landing across the room, and Mrs. Shelton collapsed.

Bonnie was just a moment behind. She pulled out her rarely used handcuffs, which had gotten more use lately than she'd expected, and with Matthew's help, secured Gerald. The man's face was bloodied from the fall. He cried and still pleaded for the ruby. Mrs. Shelton sat silently, wringing her hands.

"You watch him while I make sure this gun is safe." Bonnie was sure it was the same weapon that had killed Harvey, but it had to be handled carefully. She didn't want to contaminate whatever fingerprints might be on it. The bullets would also have to be matched. She found a zipper bag in the kitchen to hold the pistol.

As a Federal Wildlife Agent, Bonnie had the authority to make arrests—but this was really a police case. She pulled out her cell phone and dialed 911. She talked to the dispatcher, who transferred her to Chief Rogers and told him the details of what had just happened.

"Chief Rogers is on his way," Bonnie informed Matthew. "I'm going to hold Gerald until they get here to go over the crime scene."

Matthew nodded. "I'll take Mrs. Shelton out to the Hummer so she doesn't have to be in the house with him."

He helped the woman up, and they walked carefully outside.

The wolf pup remained at her feet while they waited for the police to arrive and take custody of the scene. He occasionally growled and bared his teeth at the handcuffed man.

"See? Oginali is your protector," Matthew said when he came back inside. "He was willing to take another bullet for you."

"It is almost too much to be coincidence," Bonnie conceded. "But I still think he'd have a better life with his mother and sibling. I have to try."

He shook his head. "It won't work, but I'll show you where his mother is."

"Tomorrow. We have plenty of paperwork to do this afternoon." She sighed. "Thank you for your help. I'm glad you were here. Maybe having a partner that can save my life is a good plan."

Matthew smiled. "It is the best plan."

## Chapter Twenty-three

It was a couple of days before Bonnie had the time to try taking the wolf pup back to his mother. She felt even more strongly that he deserved a chance to live like a real wolf in the wild. He had saved her life, she acknowledged. She wanted to do the same for him.

Matthew pulled his truck to a stop in the middle of an old, dirt logging road on one of the nearby mountains. The road was mostly mud from the recent snow that still clung to the pine trees.

"Oginali's mother roamed a little further uphill, but I think she's found a good den for the winter. I tracked her from where I left him the other day. It's just off a deer trail nearby. I can show you."

Bonnie was glad her new partner had been quiet on the drive up. She had been deep in thought about the wolf pup, the murders, and everything else since she'd come back to her hometown. "Thank you, but I think I need to do this by myself. I want him to stay here, and he's more likely to follow if we're both there. Just point me in the right direction."

He nodded, solemnly. The little pup was in between them on the truck's seat, panting lightly, and staring at her. "You have to do what you feel is right. That's part of your connection to nature and to the animals."

They got out of the truck, with the wolf pup following her. Matthew led her to a break in the thick forest on the passenger side, where a grassy glen opened. A small but deeply cut stream marked the change.

"Trace this creek until it levels out past the curve. One bank is steep. The other is lower. That's where his mother is making her den. It's not too far." He looked uneasy about letting her go alone.

"I'll be back soon," she promised. "I don't think there's anyone in the woods waiting to kill me." Matthew still seemed dubious. She turned to the wolf. "Come on. Follow me."

The forested side of the creek was still dark with snow-covered evergreens. Rhododendrons held the bank in place and crowded the view. The dead, brown grass and remains of tall weeds made for easier passage. The air was cold and heavy with moisture, but there was no wind.

Bonnie and the pup walked alongside the creek, through the grass. The stream curved to the right, taking them beyond Matthew's sight. Her feet were already cold, despite wearing the best boots she had for this kind of hike. She found the deer trail several yards later.

The constant trampling of hooves had created a narrow, well-worn path that crossed the stream. She turned onto the trail, the water just steps away. The creek was crusted with ice, almost completely frozen. It was wide enough to require a small leap to a steep bank leading to the heavier forest.

"Do you need help, Oginali?" she asked the wolf pup. He responded by jumping to the other side and scrambling up the bank. He looked back at her expectantly.

"I guess not," she whispered but wasn't sure if she was speaking to him or herself. She easily made her way across.

"So you like that name—Oginali?" She felt a little silly talking to the wolf as if he would reply. "And you want to be my companion?"

The wolf stopped in front of her. She nearly tripped. Oginali released a tiny, short howl that ended on a high note. He looked at her again.

The pair continued on the deer trail, as it hugged the stream. As the path moved away from the banks, the creek took a sharp turn, and the forested side dropped down to a sand bar that extended into the water. The wolf pup grumbled and ran down towards the ice, disappearing.

"Oginali!" Bonnie followed as quickly as she could.

The wolf stopped on the icy sand bar, near the water's edge. He sniffed the air, yipped a little, and turned to Bonnie as she walked up.

"Do you smell your mother?" she asked. He yipped again, with a prance and a little howl.

"Good. Good boy!" Bonnie still felt conflicted. The little wolf had saved her life. The shaman had encouraged her to accept him and maybe had brought Oginali back to the farm. Matthew had made his thoughts perfectly clear on the matter.

"Now you need to find her," she told him. "Stay with her and have your own life."

The wolf looked down from her gaze, all the joy seeming to drain from him.

"Stay here," she repeated. She turned around to start back to the truck. A gust of wind blew down the creek, causing the water to tinkle and chime against its icy rime. Oginali let out a whine, almost like a puppy. There was another, lighter gust of wind.

She turned around again, to chide him and make sure he wasn't following her.

Oginali, the wolf pup, was gone.

Matthew smiled broadly as she reappeared from the woods. "I was worried you got lost," he yelled as she approached. "The spot wasn't that far away."

She shook her head, her curly hair damp with mist and sweat. "No. It wasn't too far. Your directions were good. And the pup caught his mother's scent as we got near the sandy area in the creek bend."

"I see he listened to you. But what took you so long?"

"I was only out for twenty minutes. Twenty-five at most."

"Closer to an hour." Matthew smirked. "I was about to call in backup to search for you."

Bonnie looked at her watch, astonished to see how long she had been gone. "Being out in an unfamiliar area can do that. But the pup stayed when I told him. He had already run off when I checked back to see if he was following me."

She didn't mention the odd feeling she'd had. How

had she not noticed the time?

"That's good." He shook his head slightly and sighed. "Let's get back to the valley. I need to get ready for the parade and meet up with Thomas and Peter."

"Peter must be excited about the festivities today," Bonnie said as she climbed into the old truck. "I remember how much I loved parades when I was his age."

"You have no idea." Matthew smiled again, taking his place behind the steering wheel. "I don't know if he slept last night."

They drove out of the woods, retracing their way down the muddy, old, logging road. They talked a bit more about the parade and their plans for Christmas day.

Bonnie shivered and rubbed her arms. The truck was warming up, but she was still chilly from her hike.

"I brought some peanut butter and banana sandwiches and hot tea for lunch." Matthew handed her a big travel mug. "My grandmother mixes the tea herself from roots and herbs."

She sipped it gingerly, enjoying the extra warmth, and grabbed a sandwich. Matthew pulled off the logging road onto a paved road, heading back to the farms.

"Gerald was arrested on multiple charges—reckless endangerment, threatening a federal agent, to name a few." Bonnie said after a big bite of her sandwich. "He confessed to killing his father, and by way of that, hitting the wolf too. But Harvey had figured out something was up and swallowed the ruby at the last minute."

He nodded. "I heard the FBI is going to take him on federal charges too."

"They are preparing charges, but they're going to

wait until the local and state charges are prosecuted. There's going to be conspiracy charges too." She took a second bite.

"My brother told me the police talked to the tribal council," he started. "Gerald had accumulated some serious debts and then recently paid them off. It looks like he'd borrowed that money from a loan shark, with the promise of the ruby as collateral. They're trying to find out exactly who that was."

They finished their lunch quickly. The hot tea removed the last of the chill from her hike. Grandma Brown Elk's blend was delicious.

"Did Gerald implicate his mother or sister?" Matthew asked after a couple of quiet moments.

"No, quite the opposite. He kept them both in the dark. They didn't even know about his debts. And that was genuine shock when I told them about the ruby."

Bonnie sipped her tea and gazed out the window at the melting snow on the trees. Gerald had hurt so many people. How would the Shelton family manage to move forward now, with two members of their family taken from them? The holidays would never be the same for them.

She shook off the thoughts. "Gerald confessed he paid Vince and Ray to set the fire on the island as a way to lure Harvey out, confront him about the ruby, and then cover up his murder. Ray was having second thoughts after starting the fire. And guess what size shoe Gerald wears."

"Twelve." He finished his tea, and she nodded. "Did they ever find the rifle that was used to kill Ray?"

"It was in Vince's house. They don't know if he shot Ray to stop him from coming clean or just for a larger cut of the money from the stone. But Gerald said Vince tried to get even more money after the police interrogated him." She turned to Matthew and shook her head. "So there's another murder charge there and arson too."

"What will happen to the ruby?"

"It will be kept as evidence through the trial. Then it will go to Jean Shelton as part of Harvey's estate." But trials could take a long time. Her thoughts went back to the Sheltons and the problems Harvey's widow would have to manage now.

They turned into her driveway, and she marveled at the beauty of her home. She felt Matthew watching her for a long moment, but he didn't anything.

"So," she finally said, "see you at the parade?"

He grinned. "Wouldn't miss it."

* * *

Bonnie stood near the end of the parade route, about a block from her mom's church. The church had a big picnic shelter where the live nativity would take place. Rose Tuttle was already in the shelter helping set up. Nate Oswald was there too, dropping off his chickens and a big wooly sheep. Her mom had lamented that no one in the area had a camel. Old Man Roberts had offered one of his ostriches, but the church had politely declined.

Main Street in Christmas Tree Valley was a lazy S shape, with a big church at both ends. The general store was near the middle of the mile-long stretch. There were a couple of big houses, and a number of quaint cottage homes. Everywhere you looked, pine boughs and holly branches decorated windows, doors, and mailboxes. The trees along the road were strewn with decorations and garland.

People bundled up in warm jackets and festive hats lined both sides of the street. Children jumped up and down and yelled for Santa. Families shared hot chocolate and spiced cider. Anyone who didn't have a cup was offered one, again and again.

Bonnie sipped slowly at her own mulled apple cider with a hint of cranberry juice. She had a big Thermos full, homemade by her mom before she'd left for church. As much as she enjoyed it, she hoped Matthew would show up with more of his grandmother's special tea.

The parade started with the far church ringing its bell, and the familiar *whoop-whoop* of a police car's siren. She knew John Trump and Chief Rogers were in that first car. It would take a little while before they passed her. Two kids ran from the churchyard, each sucking on enormous candy canes, as their parents and grandfather found a place on the parade route.

Everyone in the valley must be here, she thought. Except Matthew Brown Elk. Where was he?

The flag line from the high school followed the squad car, bright green and gold Christmas flags fluttering. Of course the marching band was next, belting out mostly recognizable carols. People were still trickling in. The road was closed off, but you could still get to the church parking lots.

As the parade crawled by, the business floats and trucks were lined up next. Some of them tossed candy out to the crowd. Cell phones and cameras were lifted high by many of the revelers.

A little boy ran up next to her, pointing. It was Peter

Brown Elk. "Here she is, Dad."

She turned around and came face-to-face with Matthew.

"Merry Christmas Eve, Bonnie!" he greeted her cheerfully.

Thomas was there too, choosing his spot along the road. "Over here, Peter. You have to get ready to get some candy."

Bonnie blushed slightly, but her cheeks were already rosy from the crisp, chilly air. "Merry Christmas Eve," she repeated uncertainly. "I'm glad you made it."

Matthew was still grinning. "We would've been here earlier, but had a last-minute customer come up for a tree, so, you know...we had to make the sale."

"Of course." She nodded knowingly. "You can't let someone go without a Christmas tree."

"Did we miss the firetrucks, Edoda?" Peter asked his father.

He took a few steps to stand next to his son. "No, Atsutsa. They are near the end, just before Santa."

The boy jumped off the curb, smiling and laughing, to grab some of the candy being tossed out.

"Is your brother here?" Matthew asked.

"He is," Bonnie replied. "He's wandering around, catching up with his friends. He got in last night."

"How long is Eric staying?"

"He's going to be here for a couple days, through Christmas." Their mother was thrilled they would all be together.

A group of cloggers danced down the street, warmly dressed and smiling. Kids from the gymnastics school spun cartwheels. Bonnie had never understood how those little children could do that for a whole mile without tiring out. She didn't envy their parents when they got them home tonight. The local Rotary Club had a big banner on a pickup and handed out pamphlets. The regional hospital also had a float and gave out magnets with emergency numbers instead of candy. She was sure the kids loved that.

Matthew chatted about the people in the parade while Peter ran around, on and off the curb. Thomas excused himself to walk around the crowd.

The midpoint of the parade was the grandest float, sponsored by the Carson family and the pepper packing plant. It featured a gorgeous winter landscape with animated penguins and a decorated tree. On a throne in the center of the float was this year's Pepper Queen with a big, sparkly tiara and a warm, fluffy jacket. She smiled and waved to everyone with grace.

Bonnie finished her cup of cider and contemplated another. She was still adjusting to the cold after her time in Alabama.

"Tea?" Matthew hefted his own Thermos, noticing her empty cup.

She smiled. "Is it your grandmother's blend?"

"Of course it is. He never brings anything else." Eric Tuttle walked up as Matthew started to pour some tea. "It's good to see you, Brown Elk."

They talked for a few minutes as the classic car club rolled past then some local politicians. Finally, the Sweet Pepper Fire Brigade came into view. Peter perked up, clapping his hands. The trucks seemed larger in the growing sunset, with their red lights blazing. Every couple of minutes, one of them would blare a siren. Kids along the route screamed and covered their ears.

Everyone waved at the firefighters as they went by.

Bonnie caught eyes with Stella. She had turned down an offer to ride on the truck with the fire chief. With everything that had happened since she'd moved back to town, Bonnie just wanted to have a fun, relaxing evening with her family and her new friends. Instead, she and Stella had made plans to meet at the Nativity after the parade. She was starting to feel comfortable with her decision to be here.

The parade ended with Santa Claus on his sleigh. Elf assistants tossed out little chocolate bars. The truck that pulled the float had a red nose on the grill and antlers sticking out the windows. Parents and kids who wanted to meet Santa would have a chance after the float parked near the Nativity.

There, next to Santa, was Rose, in a bonnet and red dress with a green plaid blanket over her lap. She looked happier than Bonnie could remember, waving and smiling to children and adults alike. Her mom blew her a kiss, and she caught it. Bonnie knew these were the moments to cherish, before her family would have to face hard days of their own. She wiped away a tear with her mittened hand and laughed as Rose leaned over to give Santa a kiss, much to the crowd's delight.

Bonnie and Eric, along with Matthew and his family, walked toward the picnic shelter. Other people were working their way there too. Just as they reached the shelter, the church choir started singing. The moment became solemn as the actors played out the Nativity story. Rose Tuttle joined her children as they approached, still in her Mrs. Santa costume.

The wise men came down from the church to present their gifts. Kids started to crowd around Santa, so Thomas and Peter left to get in line. Stella Griffin and the other firefighters walked to the shelter. They had donned warm coats. The fire chief smiled and waved at Bonnie.

Rose greeted Stella with a hug. "I'm so glad you could visit with us tonight." The older lady looked beside the chief. "And, Eric, you look so handsome!"

Eric Harcourt looked at his mother. "Who are you talking to?"

"Oh, Eric," she started. "I want you to meet Eric Gamlyn." She gestured in the ghost's direction.

Her son shook his head. "Mother, there's no one—"

Stella interrupted. "Maybe we should get something to drink. Your mother has some things she needs to tell you." She whispered to the air next to her, "I know you can't drink."

"She's right, Eric. We do need to talk." Rose pulled her son by the arm.

The four pressed their way to the refreshment table near the back of the shelter, leaving Bonnie and Matthew alone. The sun finally fell beneath the horizon. She'd forgotten how quickly night came in the mountains. Thousands of Christmas lights came on, illuminating the tiny town and all the towering pine trees lining the street.

"I think we should talk too." She studied his face. His dark eyes sparkled in the outdoor lighting. "Now that we are working together…I mean, I don't know."

His smile flickered. "What is it?"

"Well, when we were out in the woods…you asked me if I wanted to go out on a date."

Matthew's gentle smile turned into a broad grin. But he was looking beyond her, over her head. She spun around, irritable at his inattention.

There, just at the edge of the light from the shelter, Dustu and his big white stag stood beside a tall, leafless oak tree. At his feet, Oginali, the wolf puppy, jumped around, yipping with delight.

Bonnie shook her head and couldn't help smiling too. She had to admit that little pup was something special. She felt Matthew's warmth behind her.

"So about that date..." he whispered.

She turned again, to face him. It was her time to stare behind him, as an older Cherokee man came striding towards them. Matthew turned to see what she was looking at.

"Elder Francis," he said reverently.

"Are you Unega Awinita?" he asked her in his thick native accent.

Bonnie wasn't sure how to respond, but Matthew nodded vigorously. It didn't matter, though, because Elder Francis acted as though he already knew the answer.

"Will you come to the reservation? One of our sacred eagles has been killed out of turn, without proper ceremony or honor. We need your expertise and the help of the white fawn."

## RECIPES

### Traditional Stollen

German sweet bread with fruit and nuts, perfect for Christmas morning

For the dough:
1 package (1/4 oz.) active dry yeast
2 tablespoons warm water (105° F)
1 cup warm milk (105° F)
3/4 cup butter, softened
1/2 cup sugar
2 eggs, lightly beaten
1/2 tablespoon grated lemon zest
1 tablespoon grated orange zest
1/2 teaspoon salt
5 cups all-purpose flour
3/4 cup raisins
1/2 cup mixed candied fruit (cherries and pineapple)
1/2 cup chopped almonds

**For the glaze:**
1 1/2 cups confectioners' sugar
2 to 3 tablespoons milk

In a large bowl, dissolve yeast in warm water. Add the milk, butter, sugar, eggs, lemon and orange zest, salt and 3 cups flour. Add the raisins, candied fruit and almonds. Add 1/2 cup remaining flour at a time, to form a soft, loose dough.

Turn dough onto a floured surface; knead until smooth and elastic, about 6-8 minutes. Use more flour if necessary. Place in a greased bowl, turning to grease top.

Cover and let rise in a warm place until doubled, about 1 1/2 hours.

Punch dough down and divide in half; cover and let rest for 10 minutes. Roll or press each half into a 12″ x 7″ oval. Fold long-wise to 1″ of opposite side; press edge lightly to seal. Place on greased baking sheets. Cover and let rise until nearly doubled, about 1 hour. Preheat oven to 375°f.

Bake loaves for 25-30 minutes or until golden brown. Cool on wire racks.

Combine confectioners' sugar and enough milk to form a thin glaze; spread over stollen.

*Yield: 2 loaves, 12-14 slices per loaf*

**Sausage and Potato Casserole with Cheese**

A light meal, great for a cold day
1 pound Italian-style sausage, cut into 1/2″ slices
1 medium onion, diced into 1/2″ pieces
1 green pepper, diced into 1/2″ pieces
4 medium potatoes, peeled and diced into 1/2 inch chunks
3-4 cloves garlic, chopped coarsely
Salt and pepper, to taste
1/2 tablespoon dried basil
1 can (14 oz.) diced tomatoes
3/4 cup mozzarella cheese
Optional: 1 or 2 jalapeno peppers, seeds removed, sliced into thin rounds

In a large skillet, brown sausage slices lightly on both sides. Drain excess grease. Preheat oven to 350°f.

Add potatoes, onions, and peppers. Sautée until potatoes are fork-tender, 15-20 minutes. Add garlic about halfway through. Drain excess grease.

Transfer sautéed ingredients to a 9″x16″ baking dish. Top with diced tomatoes, then basil, then mozzarella cheese. Bake for 10-15 minutes, until cheese is well-melted. Serve with your choice of bread.

*Serves 4*

**Almond Crescent Cookies**

A Christmas favorite, from the Sweet Pepper Café

1 cup butter, at room temperature
1 cup granulated sugar
1 teaspoon vanilla extract
2 teaspoons almond extract
2 1/3 cups all-purpose flour
1 cup ground almond meal, or almond flour
About 1 cup powdered sugar

Preheat oven to 350°f. Spray several cookie sheets with cooking spray, or line with parchment paper.

With a mixer, beat the butter and sugar until light and fluffy. Add vanilla and almond extracts, beat until incorporated.

With a wooden spoon, stir in the flour and almonds. Work mixture into a firm dough (Use your hands if necessary.) The dough will be crumbly.

Take 1 rounded tablespoon of dough, and with floured hands, roll into a log shape, thicker in the middle than the ends. Bend into a crescent shape.

Place on cookie sheets and repeat until all dough is used. Bake 12-15 minutes or until light brown.

Sift powdered sugar into a medium bowl. While the cookies are still warm, roll the crescents in the powdered sugar. Cool on racks.

*Yields 30-40 cookies*

## About the Authors

Joyce and Jim Lavene write award-winning, best-selling mystery and urban fantasy fiction as themselves, J.J. Cook, and Ellie Grant. They have written and published more than 70 novels for Harlequin, Penguin, Amazon, and Simon and Schuster along with hundreds of non-fiction articles for national and regional publications. They live in rural North Carolina with their family, their rescue animals, Quincy - cat, Stan Lee – cat, and Rudi - dog.

Visit them at:

**www.joyceandjimlavene.com**

Amazon Author Central Page:

**http://amazon.com/author/jlavene**

Made in the USA
Lexington, KY
15 August 2016